A LONG STAY IN
A DISTANT LAND

A NOVEL

A LONG STAY IN A DISTANT LAND

A NOVEL

CHIEH CHIENG

BLOOMSBURY

Published by Bloomsbury Publishing, New York and London
Distributed to the trade by Holtzbrinck Publishers

All papers used by Bloomsbury Publishing are natural, recyclable
products made from wood grown in well-managed forests.
The manufacturing processes conform to the environmental
regulations of the country of origin.

The Library of Congress has cataloged the hardcover edition as follows:

Chieng, Chieh.
A long stay in a distant land : a novel / Chieh Chieng.
p. cm.
ISBN 1–58234–533–3 (hc)
1. Chinese American families—Fiction. 2. Americans—China—Hong Kong—
Fiction. 3. Orange County (Calif.)—Fiction. 4. Hong Kong (China)—Fiction.
5. Mothers—Death—Fiction. 6. Missing persons—Fiction. 7. Young men—
Fiction. I. Title.

PS3603.H547L66 2005
813'.6—dc22
2004015078

First published in the United States by Bloomsbury Publishing in 2005
This paperback edition published in 2006

ISBN-10: 1-59691-034-8
ISBN-13: 978-1-59691-034-8

1 3 5 7 9 10 8 6 4 2

Typeset by Hewer Text Ltd, Edinburgh
Printed in the United States of America
by Quebecor World Fairfield

For my father, mother, and brother David

Table of Contents

The Lums of Orange County, California
(2002)

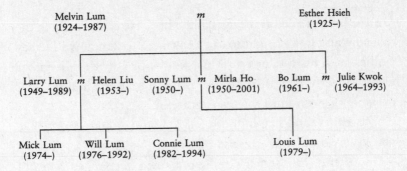

Melvin Lum (1924–1987) *m* Esther Hsieh (1925–)

Larry Lum (1949–1989) *m* Helen Liu (1953–)   Sonny Lum (1950–) *m* Mirla Ho (1950–2001)   Bo Lum (1961–) *m* Julie Kwok (1964–1993)

Mick Lum (1974–)   Will Lum (1976–1992)   Connie Lum (1982–1994)   Louis Lum (1979–)

Speaking Japanese Badly
(2002)

Louis Lum's father began calling him. He called early in the morning and late at night to say he wanted to run down Hersey Collins with his car, or crush his skull with a brick. His father never called him at work to discuss such matters, and for that measure of decorum Louis was grateful.

"Doesn't sound like a good idea," Louis would say. "Have you been riding your exercise bike?"

Day after day his father's desire remained unchanged. The old man wanted to end Hersey Collins, who five months before had fallen asleep at the wheel and crashed head-on into Louis's mother's car on a narrow stretch of Springdale Street.

"Man shouldn't have been driving," his father said. "Had no business being on the road."

Louis suggested they go to church. "It'll get you out of the house."

"I'll have to wake up Sunday morning."

"You don't sleep anyway. You'll get to be around people." The last time he had attended Golden Harvest Baptist was five years ago, and Louis wanted to return with his father now because he remembered how mellow everyone was at church. His mother had been a longstanding member of the congregation. She'd laughed and potlucked with her fellow Baptists, none

2

of whom ever expressed a desire to crack someone's neck with a hammer.

Louis hoped church would calm his father and convince him that physical violence was not the right course of action.

The old man continued calling to say, "I can't believe he's still free on the streets. I want to kill him."

Louis stopped picking up the phone. He let his machine answer his father's threats and then called back to say, "Got your message. Don't do it. Let's go to church."

His father eventually agreed to go and Louis picked him up the following Sunday. They didn't talk on the drive over.

The church was a converted barbershop located at the end of a cul-de-sac in Anaheim. The neighboring buildings housed machine and sewing shops; anyone who didn't have business on this street would have no reason to be here.

They arrived ten minutes late and sat on steel folding chairs near the back exit. In front of them were three rows of chairs facing an old wooden lectern, behind which Pastor Elkin stood. He said, "Don't be shy," and motioned for Louis and his father to come forward and sit with the rest of the congregation. Before Louis could respond, his father said, "Thanks, but we're good here."

Pastor Elkin spoke into a microphone and his voice echoed through two overhead speakers, one of which hung directly above Louis and delivered the sermon with a thumping bass.

The cement floor was flecked with sawdust left over from the parties held by the German Association of Orange County and Boy Scout Troops 145 and 167. During the week, retired Germans clinked steins and chatted here, and boys drank milk and ate brownies while music played through the speakers.

Louis's father shifted continuously throughout the hour-long service, stretching his legs, pulling them back, the steel joints of the chair whining under his weight. During the closing question-and-answer session that followed the doxology and benediction, his father stood and asked over the mostly gray heads of the twenty-five congregation members:

"If someone beat up your brother, wouldn't you feel obligated to beat him up? I've beaten up people on account of my brother. Yeah, we were kids at the time.

"If someone stole a hundred dollars from you and you had a chance to see him again, you wouldn't feel tempted to punch him? What about a slap? Because he did you wrong.

"If someone slaps you, you wouldn't slap him back? It stings, you know, to be slapped. Come on, you know you'd do it."

Each response that came back from Pastor Elkin was an unequivocal no.

No from the pastor. No from the congregation members.

No I wouldn't slap him back.

Louis fidgeted in his seat while his father posed so many variations of the same question that Pastor Elkin eventually asked, "Something you want to talk about, Sonny?"

"No," his father said, "nothing at all."

Louis's mother had brought him to church because she'd wanted him to accept Jesus into his heart. She'd said it was required for getting into Heaven. "It's like getting a passport, and once you get it you don't have to worry about going to Hell."

"If I get my passport, why do I have to keep going to church?" Louis had asked.

"Because I'm not giving you a choice."

He'd been the only child attending services filled with people in their forties and fifties. "A handsome boy," they'd say. "So smart."

4

"Not so bright," his mother would respond. "Terrible in geography. Doesn't know Cameroon from Ghana." Once she'd said, "Looks too much like his grandfather. His paternal grandfather."

"Why do you tell them I'm creepy looking?" he'd asked on the drive home.

"I was being humble for you," his mother said, her eyes fixed on the road.

"If they want to say I'm handsome, why do you have to say I look creepy?"

"You don't look creepy. People will like you more if you don't accept their praise. If you tell them you're slow-witted and clumsy, they'll think you're the opposite."

"They'll think I'm slow-witted and clumsy."

"It's called humility."

Louis believed church had been like a party for his mother and she hadn't wanted to attend alone. She'd press his Sunday suit Saturday night and slick his hair with gel Sunday morning.

His father should have been the one to sacrifice his Sunday mornings to accompany her, but she said, "He decided long ago he'd be happy in Hell. You know what he said? He said, 'I'd go straight to Hell in exchange for sleeping in Sundays for the rest of my life. Do you have any idea how tired I am by the time I get to Sunday?'

"I said, 'Hey buddy, you're not the only one who works fifty-plus hours a week. You don't have to stay up nights prepping for lectures. You don't have to grade exams on your weekends.'

"He told me to stop nagging him, and I was only trying to do him a favor."

When, as a child, Louis asked his father to go to church, he answered, "Why should I?" and his mother said, "Don't nag him. He wants to go to Hell."

Louis had asked his father to go so he himself could sleep in. More important, he hadn't wanted his father to go to Hell.

He first heard Pastor Elkin's sermon on damnation when he was seven. Pastor Elkin had described the Underworld as a place where eternal flames melted the skin off your body, on which baseball-sized boils swelled and exploded, jetting out thick streams of greasy black pus onto the black streets, where packs of the wild dead—with their eternally melting skin and continuously erupting boils—hunted down and vomited on each other.

"Now don't you want Jesus to come into your heart?" his mother asked on the drive home.

That night he prayed, "Jesus, please come into my heart." He made the same request every night for six months, and asked Pastor Elkin if there was a limit to how many times he could do it. "I'm sure once is enough," Pastor Elkin said. Louis didn't believe him and continued inviting Jesus until the end of the year.

Jesus, he believed, was someone who looked like Max von Sydow, who handed out fish and bread to new arrivals, and who said, "See, I told you so," as they passed through what Pastor Elkin had described as gates laden with pearls and silver.

The day after high school graduation, Louis announced he was finished with church. "I invited Jesus into my heart three hundred and twenty-four times," he told his mother. "I'm going to Heaven." Saturday had been his only day to sleep in and he wanted his Sunday mornings back.

"You're eighteen and I can't force you to keep going," she said. She was upset and disappointed and he felt bad for her.

However, the next Sunday he slept in until noon and woke up to one of the most refreshing and happy Sundays he'd ever had.

In the five years since he'd last attended Golden Harvest with her, no one new had joined the congregation, which now consisted of the same twenty-five people week in and week out.

The youngest members looked at least fifty. Many looked sixty and over. Louis felt like he was watching a species in its final years, the last clan of Atlantic seabirds being killed off by hunters, oil spills, or simply time, until there was not one left and no evidence they'd ever existed.

There were never curious visitors who happened to drop in. There were no children and no one who seemed capable of a short sprint, or even a light jog around the block. Hairs were gray and silver, skin was cracked, and life was always a burst blood vessel away from ending.

At the end of each service, Pastor Elkin would say, "Let us continue trying to bring in new sheep," and the congregation would say, "Amen."

A month into their churchgoing, Louis's father ran into congregation member Arnold Mannion at an Albertson's and asked him a question.

Arnold said there was no way he'd ever slap somebody back.

"You're not being honest," Louis's father said.

"You can slap me if you want."

"Are you serious?"

"Please," Arnold said.

"He told me to," Louis's father said on the drive to Golden Harvest the following Sunday. "He put his groceries down and waited for me to do it."

"What happened?" Louis asked.

7

"I slapped him."

"Hard?"

"There was a loud pop. His faced turned pink. I didn't hit him that hard. He has delicate skin."

"Wasn't he mad?"

"No. He hugged me. He said, 'Good, get your grief out.' Then he smiled." Louis's father looked puzzled. "What kind of a person asks to get slapped and smiles after?"

Louis shrugged and kept his eyes on the road ahead.

The church members often related personal testimonies that involved the importance of forgiveness. At each service, someone stood in front of the congregation and told a story about how he'd invited for dinner a coworker who'd "borrowed" his soda from the company fridge, or how he'd brought apple fritters to a neighbor whose dogs crapped on his front lawn.

That morning, Arnold stood and delivered his testimony. "Sonny Lum slapped me last week. I was happy to help him vent his frustration."

Pastor Elkin nodded.

Louis's father stood from his seat in the back and shouted, "He asked me to do it! It was consensual!"

"That's right," Arnold said, and cries of "Sweet Jesus!" and "Yes Lord!" echoed through the room.

"Nobody's blaming you," Pastor Elkin told Louis's father. "Arnold wanted to help you. He asked you to vent your frustration because he hoped it would make you feel better."

"He can slap me back," Louis's father said. "He has the right. Come on, Arnold, you know you want to."

Louis pulled his father back down.

"What kind of a church is this?" his father asked on the drive home. He was disappointed to learn that Golden Harvest would not deviate from the forgiveness of the New Testament, the turning-the-other-cheek rule. It would forever consider eye-for-an-eye an invalid and unjustifiable formula for present-day life, and because of this Louis's father decided to stop attending. The next Sunday Louis slept well past noon.

Louis was making a living as an editorial assistant at a hot rod magazine based in Mission Viejo, and the salary afforded rent for a studio apartment in Santa Ana, utilities, car insurance, gas, and food, with twenty dollars left over each month.

Two years ago, he'd graduated from college and taken the job mostly because it was all he could get and partly to annoy his mother.

"Nineteen a year?" she'd asked. "You have a college degree." She'd believed having a B.A. meant working for no less than thirty a year. "This is insulting," she'd said.

He hadn't felt insulted, but her resistance to his job had heightened his enjoyment of it. He found satisfaction in doing or saying things she didn't want him to do or say. He would never have taken a job to rile anyone else, though now that she was dead, he felt he should have found something with a higher salary and a more respectable title. He could use the extra money. He could use a vacation. A quiet room in a distant land. A long stay to forget about Hersey, the accident, and his father's rage. He wanted to sleep on foreign soil, somewhere where nobody knew him and he knew nobody—Auckland, Toronto, Yonkers.

He was a fact checker and he did his job well. The copy chief handed him so many EA of the Month awards that he was eventually declared the permanent EA of the Month. His picture hung on the wall in the front lobby under a giant portrait of

Percy, the Chihuahua that belonged to the publisher's wife. In addition, he was assigned a leather reclining chair with oak armrests. It was the most luxurious chair ever given to an EA. All the others had standard-issue rollers with synthetic fabric and poor back support.

Louis's mother had lived by the code "Whatever you do, do it better than everyone else who's doing it, or find something else to do." A week before the accident, they'd spoken on the phone and he'd told her about his chair.

"It's the best chair for someone in your position?" she'd asked.

"Yes."

"Leather, you said?"

"Yes."

"Better than nothing."

Two weeks after quitting Golden Harvest, Louis's father called and said, "I'm driving to his house. I have a knife. I'm going to stab him in the heart." It was one in the morning, and the old man wasn't being rude by calling because neither of them went to bed before two or three.

"You sure you want to do this?" Louis asked.

"Yes."

"Really?"

"Yes."

"You really going to his house?"

"No. But I plan to."

"You're home?"

"Yes."

"I'll come over."

"I'm really thinking about going there. I can do it."

"I know. Stay right there."

Hersey Collins was a twenty-seven-year-old first-year resident at UCI Medical driving home after a forty-eight-hour shift when he nodded out. The wheel had slipped from his fingers and turned his car directly into her path. The total strength of impact had equaled their velocities combined, eight thousand pounds of steel and glass crashing at one hundred miles an hour. He'd been lucky. He'd been driving the much bigger car, a gray Land Cruiser that'd crushed her Camry. The paramedics had found her body in the backseat, along with the steering wheel and most of the dash.

Louis arrived at his father's house and found him sitting on the driveway, wearing a white T-shirt, gray sweats, and sandals.

"I have to do something to him." His father stood and walked back into the house. Louis followed. "You retiled the hallway."

"Took a few weeks," his father said.

"It looks nice." Louis walked into the living room. "You repainted the walls."

"Yeah."

The carpet had been replaced by dark brown hardwood.

"I shouldn't have called," his father said. "You can go home."

"You can't just call, tell me what you told me, and tell me to go home."

"I'm fine."

Louis was angry at Hersey's carelessness, but he had no desire to kill the man. What Hersey shouldn't have done was wait for Louis's father at the hospital, offer his apologies, address, and number, and say, "If there's anything I can do for you, I'll do it." He should have gone home.

"Sorry I woke you," Louis's father said.

"Say, 'I won't kill Hersey Collins.'"

His father said nothing.

"You never said you were driving to his house before," Louis said.

"I was trying to work myself up."

"Is my bed still here?"

"Yes."

"I'll sleep here tonight."

They got up for work the next morning, and Louis came back at four sharp to make sure his father returned soon after. They watched TV that evening, and repeated this pattern of work and TV until the end of the week, when he asked his father, "Do you still want to kill him?"

"Yes."

Another week passed.

Each time Louis asked the question, his father said, "Yes."

"If you say you won't drive to his house, even if you want to, I'll leave," Louis said. "I'll go back to my place."

"I don't want to lie."

"Don't you want this house back to yourself?"

His father didn't answer.

"Why do you want to do it? What good would it do?"

"It's like he cut off my right leg," his father said. "And now I'm hobbling around and he's walking fine with two good legs."

"A leg?" Louis asked. His father, at fifty-two, had thick thighs left over from a lifetime of cycling. Since the old man stopped exercising, his formerly sculpted quadriceps had softened into loose mounds of flesh. A film of dust covered the stationary bike in the garage.

Pastor Elkin called to invite them back to church, and it was fortunate that Louis's father screened his calls. Pastor Elkin or a church member would speak through the answering machine:

"Just saying hi."

"We miss you. Would love to have you back."

"Sonny, this is Arnold. Please don't feel bad about slapping me. Nobody blames you for it."

Louis and his father took to raiding the fridge at one or two in the morning. They'd grunt, hand the other a loaf of bread or a box of cereal, and then retreat to their rooms. In bed, Louis played his Nintendo video games or read comic books starring Godzilla and Gamera. These were childhood things he'd dug up from the corner of the garage, where his parents had hidden them because of their Japanese origins.

His parents had disliked all things Japanese because the government of Japan, they said, refused to admit to killing ten million Chinese during World War II. And the Japanese, his mother said, filched thousands of Chinese characters for their kanji. "Half their language is ours," she'd said. "They should call it Chinese Two."

But she'd never had a problem with Doug Inouye, who'd cut and permed her hair for over ten years. The friend she'd visited most often had been Sheila Yamada. She'd often said of these two, "They're not Japanese. They don't even speak it." And that had been an important distinction to her. Because they didn't speak Japanese, Doug Inouye and Mrs. Yamada were good people. Because she could speak Cantonese and Mandarin, and read and write Chinese, Louis's mother felt entitled to as much anger as Mrs. Wah, who'd lost her parents under the Japanese occupation.

Louis's mother met Mrs. Wah during a three-week tour of southern China. She was the guide, and would tell Louis's mother during meals or on the bus what she thought of the Japanese. "If I hadn't already been in Hong Kong, I'd be dead,"

Mrs. Wah said. She talked about how the Japanese soldiers had tied people to stakes and flayed them with swords. She talked about Japanese doctors who'd vivisected captured civilians, slicing open their chests and prying their ribs apart. She talked about Unit 731, which had detonated grenades inches from people to test the effects of grenades detonated inches from people.

Louis's mother usually brought up Japanese atrocities at dinner, and his father would say, "No talking. You two are making me lose my appetite."

"Everybody's done something to everybody else," Louis would say.

"Example?" his mother would ask.

"The Mongols invaded Japan in the thirteenth century."

"They didn't dissect live people."

"The Chinese invaded and occupied Vietnam for a thousand years."

"They didn't slice out their lungs and livers while they screamed."

"The Americans wiped out the Indians with diseases that made them puke their intestines."

"They didn't—"

"Dinner's for eating," his father would say. "Children are starving in Mozambique right now. They would love to have food. Shut up!"

It'd disappointed his parents greatly when Louis began watching the subtitled Japanese family drama *Love Hurts* each Sunday afternoon. Passing through the living room on their way to the yard or garage, they would urge him to change the channel.

"Turn to *The Three Stooges*. It's a better show.

"Go outside.

"Play with your friends.

"Make some friends, then."

They found things to do during the show. They took walks around the neighborhood. His mother tended plants in the garden and his father sat in the garage, studying the water heater like he'd one day fix it if it ever broke.

The show's main character was a twelve-year-old boy named Toshi who learned life lessons in each episode: *Grandpapa's sick and can't make the neighborhood go tournament? Yoshi! No problem. Toshi puts on Grandpapa's robes, wears a fake beard, and plays in his stead, winning a brand-new pair of sandals. But he has to give them back because he lied. Lying's not acceptable.*

After Toshi learned his lesson, he was punished by his father offscreen. This happened toward the end of every episode. Armed with a bamboo stick, Toshi's father would lead his son into the boy's bedroom. The screen would fade out and then fade back to reveal the two fishing by a river or washing the dishes, smiles on their faces.

Arigato, Papa! Thank you for teaching me not to dress up like Grandpapa, and for showing me that deception never achieves a good result.

It'd never occurred to Louis before he started watching the show that one could be grateful for and excited about getting smacked on the ass. But there was Toshi getting beat and loving it, always smiling afterward as if it'd been the most delightful thing that'd ever happened to him.

When Louis was being reprimanded by his parents, when he wanted to annoy them, or when he wanted to show them he was nothing like them, he'd speak the language of the show. He'd combine words, mix together parts of different words, and speak a tongue that was as much his as it was Japanese.

15

At the dinner table:

"Why a C plus in geography? We bought you a new globe. Forty-five dollars."

"Nani?"

"In English or Chinese. And tell me why a C plus in geography? Well? Name two countries that border Libya."

"Yakisobadeshita."

"Stop it."

"Warewarewa. Warewaremashita."

"You're asking for it." His mother would pick up the Ping-Pong paddle she kept constantly near. She did not play Ping-Pong.

"Arigato!"

Louis never enjoyed the punishments as much as Toshi. Speaking Japanese meant his mother whacking him with the paddle, resulting in a degree of pain that was not worth speaking Japanese, badly or otherwise.

Toshi was an idiot for giving thanks after being punished. Righteous punishment did not exist, because the snap of a wooden paddle against one's flesh, endured for whatever reason, whether for the sake of education or correction, was not right. It hurt like hell.

When Hersey Collins said, "If there's anything I can do for you, I'll do it," he wasn't volunteering to be stabbed in the heart.

His father needed to remember, and remember correctly. Mirla Lum had been a math professor at Cal State Fullerton, a Baptist who'd wanted to go to Heaven, a daughter, a wife, and a mother.

Lying in his old bed in his father's house, Louis's chest tightened. *"Warewarewa,"* he said. *"Warewarewa,"* he said louder, recalling the sting of the paddle, the blue veins on his mother's unfortunately strong hands. *"Warewarewa!"* He saw her face full of anger and life.

The hallway floor creaked. The boards groaned under the mass of his father's body, twenty pounds overweight.

A knock.

Louis got out of bed. He opened the door and looked his father in the eyes.

"You okay?" his father asked.

"She's not a fucking leg."

A Relentless Rain of Steel Death
(2002)

Louis's family, based in Orange County since Grandpa Melvin and Grandma Esther migrated south from San Francisco over forty years ago, had recurring problems with death.

It seemed that every time Louis saw his relatives, it was to make burial arrangements for another Lum who'd passed away suddenly, unexpectedly.

The rash of deaths Louis attributed to his grandfather, whom he knew mostly from a framed black-and-white photo that sat in his father's bedroom. Grandpa was a man in his mid-thirties with a black suit, a broad square face, and a thin, pointed nose.

According to Grandma, Grandpa had fought in World War II. Amid the scattered cinder blocks of demolished French towns, he'd unleashed a relentless rain of steel death with his U.S. Army–issued Browning M1919A4. Grandma's exact words had been "Grandpa served in France." Louis's father had said, based on what Grandma had told him when he was a child, "Grandpa liberated French villages and fed starving children. He shot lots of Nazis."

Louis knew his Grandma had meant "relentless rain of steel death." That was how he'd described it in a twenty-page family history report he'd written in the seventh grade, and that was how he'd always seen it—a hail of machine-gun bullets tearing flesh and bone and Grandpa's finger at the trigger.

Grandpa had violated the fundamental law that one should not kill another. He'd had a choice. He could have chosen not to join the war and not to shoot people.

For every man Grandpa had killed, Death had designated a Lum to be picked off. Death was a very real being who shared Louis's father's desire for equality through revenge, forever seeking an eye for an eye. In Louis's mind, Death looked like Grandpa from that black-and-white photo.

Louis's cousin Mick was skeptical. "No such thing as a family death curse," he'd said. "And what do you mean by a death curse? We're all going to die anyway."

"We're all going to die from unnatural causes," Louis said.

"Bullshit."

"Bruce Lee and his son were cursed. They died in their prime."

"They were unlucky, like our family. That's all. If you keep thinking you're going to fall down a flight of stairs, it'll happen."

"That might happen," Louis said.

"It won't happen if you don't think about it. Stop thinking about dying, jackass. Think about what you're going to have for lunch tomorrow."

"That's what you think about?" Louis asked.

"I know exactly what I'm eating tomorrow," Mick said.

"What is it?"

"A salad, no dressing. An orange. Two quarter-pound cheeseburgers, pickles and tomatoes only. Two glasses of water, each with a slice of lime."

Louis never discussed the curse with anyone except Mick. He didn't think his father and grandmother would appreciate him placing the burden of death on Grandpa, but he knew Death watched him each day through crosshairs. Even now he waited at least seven seconds before crossing a street on a green, never ordered anything with meat at fast food restaurants, and checked multiple times to make sure his stovetops were off before leaving the apartment or going to bed.

He knew he could be struck down at any time. He had a will. He had, along with each member of his family except Mick—who refused to believe he'd die before the age of seventy—a life insurance policy.

And he always remembered the Lums who'd passed away in his lifetime:

—December 2001, Mom, fifty-one, head-on collision with Hersey Collins's car;

—May 1994, his cousin Connie, twelve, complications from *E. coli* bacteria found in a bacon cheeseburger purchased at a fast food restaurant;

—August 1993, Aunt Julie, twenty-nine, stomach cancer;

—October 1992, his cousin Will, sixteen, heatstroke during high school football practice;

—March 1989, Uncle Larry, forty, fell off a cliff in Mammoth while skiing;

—June 1987, Grandpa Melvin, sixty-two, struck by an ice cream truck while crossing the street.

Each year the Lums convened for a family meeting. The specific date varied depending on whether a person had died or what day Grandma deemed appropriate for a gathering. She often picked a day in the spring, when she felt the weather was particularly sunny and warm.

"When is it not sunny and warm here?" Uncle Larry once

asked. "Let's meet in October next year. I don't do anything in October."

Grandma's dining room had beige carpet and bare beige walls. They'd sit at the dining table under a chandelier that resembled an inverted pincushion. She often played music before the start of each meeting as she waited for late arrivals to file in. Louis and his parents usually arrived on time, hoping everyone else would also, allowing for a quick meeting. Uncle Larry and his family always arrived late.

While waiting, they'd eat the food Grandma had prepared, usually egg rolls and fried turnip cakes with diced onions and shrimp, while Bessie Smith and Billie Holiday sang through the living room speakers.

In between songs, she'd encourage them to eat more and Louis's parents would compliment her on how beautifully she'd decorated the room. Louis would eat and drink while Lady Day's "Everything I Have Is Yours" or "I Hadn't Anyone Till You" played. The music served its primary purpose, standing in for conversation and filling the room while Louis's father whispered in his mother's ear, "What time is it? It's only been five minutes? *You* eat another turnip cake."

Grandma used the meetings to make sure each family member was in good health. She'd ask any combination of the following questions: "Have you had a serious illness this past year? Are you ill now? Are you happy? Is there anything I can help with? Is there anything you want that you don't have or can't get?"

She'd stare at her grandchildren until they said, "Grandma, you're making me nervous. I'm not sick."

At the meeting to discuss Connie's funeral arrangements, Aunt Helen arrived to the sounds of a harp being played over a waterfall. This was during Grandma's two-year nature period, when she listened to nothing but instrumental music accompanied by the sounds of nature, which included chirping crickets, rustling leaves, and rushing streams.

"Why the damn racket?" Aunt Helen asked.

"I'll turn it down," Grandma said. After that meeting she stopped playing music and Louis waited in silence for the rest of his relatives to arrive.

Following Connie's death, Aunt Helen officially dropped Lum off her name, saying to Grandma, "This family is cursed," to which Louis silently said, Amen.

But she showed up every year, and this Louis interpreted as a sign of respect for Grandma or the fact that Aunt Helen didn't have anywhere else to go. Both her parents were dead, she had no siblings, she was a widow, and she had just one remaining child. He didn't blame her for changing her name.

Aunt Helen asked Mick to change his name as well, but he refused. "There's no curse," he said. "Change your name back to Lum."

Louis knew what Mick wouldn't acknowledge, that changing a name would serve no good purpose. Death had a long memory. He knew who was who.

Louis was born of Sonny, who was born of Melvin, machine gunner in World War II. This was his history, as true as fact, as true as the fact that he was now stuck in his father's house. His lease had expired and he'd moved back in with the old man, who wouldn't stop thinking about killing Hersey Collins.

They didn't talk. They were mired in a mutual silent treatment that began after he had told his father two months earlier that his mother wasn't a fucking leg. They avoided words whenever possible. A grunt uttered deep from his father's chest meant "I'm home. How was your day?"

Louis's "Ehhh" meant "All right, thanks for asking."

Louis's "Huhff" meant "I'm cooking dinner now. Would you like some?"

His father tapping a cup with a spoon meant "I'm having some juice. You want me to pour you a cup, too?"

Louis rapping the dinner table with his knuckles meant "Dinner's ready. I said dinner's ready!"

His father pounding a fist against the kitchen counter meant "You left the tap running! Do you want to use up all the water in southern California? Why do you turn on the tap and then leave the kitchen? And you pounded the counter on me for doing the same thing yesterday, after I poured you a cup of juice!"

According to Grandma, the first Lum family meeting took place in 1943, when Grandpa announced he was enlisting in the army.

Preparations for the latest Lum family meeting began when the phone rang on a Friday night in August 2002. Louis and his father were eating cereal and watching TV. They were sitting on opposite ends of the couch, separated by the space of one whole cushion. A rap music video was playing, and Louis and his father let the phone ring.

Louis was first exposed to rap when he was ten. His mother had gone out one Saturday morning and his father had said, "Turn off those cartoons. They'll destroy your mind. I want you to listen to something. It's an important part of our culture and speaks of the oppression of colored people in this country."

He retrieved a stash of vinyl records from the garage and carefully slipped one out of its case. He wiped both sides of the record with a tissue, then placed it gingerly on the player.

The song was N.W.A.'s "Fuck Tha Police," and he began mouthing the lines, hopping from foot to foot, swinging his head like a ball on a car antenna. "Isn't this better than your grandmother's music?" he asked.

Louis remembered what Pastor Elkin had said about demonic possession. "It begins with uncontrollable gyrations and an awkward flailing of limbs. A man possessed speaks an ancient, indecipherable language. For example, *Yaka-ah-way mana Beelzebub* means 'I serve the dark lord Beelzebub.'"

By the time Louis's father shouted something about a young nigger going on a warpath that consequently resulted in a bloodbath, Louis was so certain his father's body had been commandeered by fallen angels that he ran screaming out the front door, the old man yelling after him, "I'm trying to teach you some culture! Come back!"

After he moved back in with his father, Louis felt the bass pumping from the speakers in the old man's room and pulsing through his wall like a heartbeat, and in place of his father's voice, lyrics featuring Dre and Eazy.

The phone rang and rang until the machine picked up and Grandma Esther spoke. There was a tremble in her voice Louis wasn't accustomed to hearing. He'd never even seen her cry.

"Sonny, come to my house tomorrow," she said. "I need to see you. Bo's missing."

New Territory
(1962)

Weekday afternoons Esther rocked Bo on the square concrete patio of her Garden Grove home. She enjoyed the weight of his chin on her shoulder, the warm drool wetting her clothes, the heft of his thighs like small sacks of baking powder. She sat for hours with Bo in the shade of a large umbrella while Melvin was at work doing other people's taxes and Larry and Sonny were at school.

Weekends Melvin stayed in the garage cleaning and polishing his old army uniform and shell casings, and Sonny and Larry scoured the streets on their bicycles like a couple of cats. The boys would ride out with empty paper grocery bags and come back hours later, their bags filled with cookies, candies, and other food donated by neighbors.

A year younger than Larry, Sonny led the way, having planned their day's route through the various houses in the neighborhood. Afterward, he inspected and divided their spoils.

"Oatmeal and chocolate both count as pastries," Sonny said in defense of grabbing two chocolate bars for himself. "You got three bags of oatmeal. I prefer the oatmeal, but I want you to have it. It keeps you regular, which means it keeps your face clear of acne. Chocolate can give you cancer. Uncle Phil told me about research that proves it. I don't want you to get sick."

For weeks afterward and despite Esther's prodding, Larry would not eat chocolate for fear of cancer. He took Sonny's word over hers.

She was disappointed that one, Sonny was exploiting his gullible older brother, and two, the boys preferred treats from outside the home over treats she'd provided.

Even after she bought cookies and candies and stored them in bright red jars in the kitchen, the boys continued going out for food.

She thought Melvin would tell them to stop, but he shrugged when she showed him a pack of gum confiscated from the children.

"Impressive," he said, sitting on his stool, holding a white rag in one hand and a bullet in the other. It looked like a plain lead .22 caliber, about the size of a thumb, and it glinted under the garage's lone sixty-watt bulb.

"That's all you're going to say?" she asked, upset that because of him, she knew what a plain lead .22 caliber looked like.

"That's what I said to them," he said.

"They already showed you?"

"Yeah."

"You encouraged this?"

"They planned it out themselves. I was just cheering them on."

"What kind of children are you raising here?" she asked.

"Self-reliant ones."

She stared at him and the longer she stared, the more unfamiliar he became, the way her face turned into a stranger's if she stared at a photo of herself long enough. She tried to find something in his face to help her understand why he didn't care that their sons were spending practically all their free time outside the house.

"What?" he asked.

"Nothing."

She lectured her boys. "You aren't orphans. Anything you two want, you ask me or your father. You don't go around begging. How does that make me look? Yes, your father also said no. Roll your eyes again, Sonny, and I will slap the dimples off your face."

Whenever she ran into Mrs. Walker or Mrs. Alphonse at the market, they would say, "Sonny and Larry stopped by last weekend. They're so cute. I love the dimples on your younger one." Mrs. Walker once said, "And their hair. It's such a dark black."

Mrs. Walker and Mrs. Alphonse were the widows of the neighborhood and the women the boys visited most often. These women, like everyone else in Orange County with the exception of the Lums, were white. Moving to southern California had been Esther's idea. Orange County had been Melvin's. He'd always insisted on being a lone Chinese man in a sea of white, whether in France or California.

Chinatown was just thirty miles north in Los Angeles. She'd grown up happily in San Francisco's Chinatown and missed it. Chinatowns were where the Chinese should live in this country. If the boys rode their bicycles around Chinatown, they could visit people who spoke Cantonese and offered them egg tarts and dried prunes.

Dark black hair! she thought. Her children were parading around the neighborhood for treats like a couple of albino tigers at the circus. They were not exotic. They were disobedient children.

It angered Esther that the boys were spending more time with these women than with her. When had she ever given them the

27

impression that they weren't welcome at home, that they needed to wander the neighborhood like a couple of gypsies? What did they see in these women that she lacked?

Even if they were happier outside, they had an obligation to stay home and be unhappy. This was the definition of family, that you are beholden to people not of your choosing. And even the people you did choose, like your husband, you really didn't choose. Because the person you married was not the person you were married to.

When she married Melvin, she did not know he was the sort of man who would leave her, willingly and enthusiastically, to fight a war on the other side of the world. She did not know he was the sort of man who would prefer the company of brass shells over his family.

And for the ones you didn't choose, those surprises who came out of your body and announced with cries and tears their presence to the world—as if they had endured some kind of pain during your labor—you raised and fed and gave all the affection you could muster, with the very reasonable expectation that they not go to someone else for food.

"What's wrong with the cookies here?" she asked.

"They're too easy," Sonny said.

"Easy?"

"It's right there on the counter," Sonny said. "There's no challenge. Food earned through work is twice as tasty as food lying in a jar waiting to be eaten."

Larry nodded.

"Who taught you that? Your father?"

The boys said nothing, which meant yes.

"No more treats," she said. "Even if they insist, you don't take any. It's wrong. It's dishonorable to take something and give nothing in return."

"We give these people the joy of our company," Sonny said. "We water their plants and help clean up their yards. We tell them stories."

"About what?"

"About school," Sonny said. "Softball and math quizzes."

"And they give you food for these stories?"

"Yes. And we tell them jokes."

"Like what?"

"Knock knock," Sonny said.

"What?"

"You're supposed to say, 'Who's there?'" Sonny said.

"Why?"

"Knock knock."

Esther sighed. "Who's there?"

"Sonny," Sonny said. "Now you're supposed to say, 'Sonny who?'"

"Why?"

"Just say it."

Esther sighed again. "Sonny who?"

"Sonny Lum."

"What's funny about that?" Esther asked.

"I made that one up myself," Sonny said.

"That's a good one," Larry said.

"Thanks," Sonny said.

"They've got nothing to do anyway," Larry said.

"Who're they?" Esther asked.

"Mrs. Walker and Alphonse," Sonny said. "They like listening. Anything we say is funny to them."

"Good point," Larry said.

"Thanks," Sonny said.

"From now on," she said, "everything you eat comes from this house."

They promised her they'd obey, but she began discovering peanut shells and torn Bazooka gum wrappers in the trash. This prompted her to search them after they returned from their bike rides.

"Against the wall," she'd say. They'd spread their legs and raise their arms, and she'd frisk them the way Lee Marvin patted down cornered suspects on *M Squad*.

"Good afternoon, Fascist Woman," Melvin would say if he happened to pass by. The boys would giggle.

She soon stopped searching them because they would continue eating their cookies and candies outside the house. They'd find places to bury caches of food. They'd stuff themselves to their hearts' content elsewhere and learn to stop bringing evidence home.

She called Mrs. Walker and Mrs. Alphonse. "I know you're feeding my kids. I put them on a strict diet. One cookie makes a difference. One cookie makes a hell of a difference, so stop it!"

Her conversations with them at the market became shorter.

"I didn't feed them," Mrs. Walker would say.

"They didn't come by," Mrs. Alphonse would say. "I swear."

"Good-bye," they'd say.

Bo was her last chance. He was the one who'd stay by her side. When she rocked him on the patio, she felt they were the only two people in the world. No Sonny. No Larry. No Melvin. No in-laws, friends, and acquaintances. "You'll never go somewhere else for candy, will you?" she'd ask, and he'd burp or grin in response.

More Foreign than the Foreigners
(1975)

They observed a moment of silence before eating, but it was
not to pray, not to thank, not to be grateful for, and not to
remember. It was a moment they'd replayed every evening for
the past year, a moment of approximately thirty seconds, but
stretched to a seemingly endless length of time by Bo's nervous,
growling stomach and his anxious glances at anything and
anyone not Melvin, who gave Bo this one moment to put his
plate, spoon, and fork back in the kitchen cabinet and drawers
and to "eat like a goddamn normal person, using a goddamn
normal rice bowl and chopsticks."

Esther hated when her husband cursed in front of Bo.

"Let's get started already," she said.

Melvin snatched a cauliflower from a center dish with his
chopsticks and waved the vegetable at Bo. "Do you even
remember how to use this anymore?"

"Stop fooling around," Esther said.

"I'm asking him a question." Melvin popped the cauliflower
in his mouth. He often complained that Bo at fourteen was
skinnier and shorter than either of his brothers had been at the
same age.

This boy and his infatuation with the Rolling Stones, English-
men as scrawny as he was. This boy who stayed up nights

reading comic books, this boy who holed up in his room on weekends instead of going outside, who wouldn't eat rice from a bowl, much less pick up food with chopsticks.

Bo's preference for the fork and plate had driven Melvin mad, and kept Esther up at night listening to his madness.

He was skinny, Melvin said, because he wasn't eating with the right utensils, because the flow of his food intake had been disrupted by the steely fork that speared and deformed vegetables mercilessly, the inflexible spoon that could not pluck and pick meat with the precision and grace of a pair of chopsticks, which were themselves extensions of one's fingers, and the flat, rigid plate that could not hold rice the way a bowl did, in a compact and easily accessible mound that retained both heat and flavor.

"You're confounding your stomach! Your body can't handle it!" he'd shout in the middle of a meal, surprising Bo into dropping his fork or spoon, the steel clanking against the plate.

What kind of man would Bo become, Melvin asked, if he didn't eat with chopsticks and didn't go outside on weekends? What kind of a boy avoided the sun like a vampire?

He was convinced that Bo was something foreign, a genetic tangent, a hiccup in the bloodline. His other sons had never acted this way. Bo was more foreign than the Germans who thought sausage and pickled cabbage were such fine stuff, the English who boiled the flavor out of anything that had flavor, and the Indians with their one-trick-pony curry.

This boy looked Chinese and had his name, but he was more foreign than all the foreigners Melvin had ever met.

Esther listened to her husband's grievances in bed. She learned to nod her head in agreement because if she called him an idiot or wrong, he'd ask, "How am I an idiot?" or "How am I wrong?"

and would not let her sleep until she explained herself to his satisfaction. And he was never satisfied with her reasons for calling him an idiot or wrong, reasons that included, "Because I said so," "Because you are," and "Because I said you are."

Neither Melvin nor Bo realized how much they had in common. They were the only two people Esther knew to have put so much thought into the act of eating. As long as she had enough to fill her stomach, she didn't care how the food got in, whether via chopsticks, a fork, or a shovel.

And what was the boy's explanation? Melvin asked. Efficiency. *Efficiency!*

Bo had explained his desire for efficiency the first night he brought a clean, white plate of rice to the table.

"I gave you a bowl," Melvin said.

"I want to use this," Bo said.

"For what purpose?" Melvin asked.

"To hold my rice."

"Your bowl holds your rice," Melvin said.

"I can give you another bowl if yours is dirty," Esther said.

Melvin put his hand up. "Wait. I think something's going on here." He looked at Bo's plate. "What's wrong with the bowl?"

"It's too small."

"It holds enough rice to fill me up." Melvin patted his paunch, which had grown considerably in recent years. "And I can eat a lot more than you can."

"I have to refill the bowl with rice two, even three times for just one dinner," Bo said. "I have to constantly pick vegetables and meat from the center dishes as I eat. With my own plate, I can pile on all the food at one time. Then I won't have to waste energy refilling. I can shorten my dinner by about ten minutes. It's more efficient this way."

"Part of the fun is picking up food as you go along." Melvin nodded at the three center plates that held broccoli, *ong choi*, and shrimp. He plucked a shrimp with his chopsticks and waved it in front of Bo's face. "See? Fun." He ate it, then picked up a few pieces of the *ong choi*, twirling the stringy greens around his chopsticks. "I never know what I'll want next." He chewed and swallowed. "Maybe I'm in the mood to eat more shrimp. Or more vegetables. I'll go with shrimp. There. See? Freedom to choose what I eat, constantly adjusting the ratio of meat to vegetable instead of having it all smashed together on a plate. What if I'm feeling meaty? Then a standard plate of equal meat and vegetable just won't do. Or what if I'm feeling like vegetables? What if I change my mind *in the middle of the meal*?" He plucked another shrimp. "The chopsticks are a tool of democracy."

"The bowl and chopsticks are obsolete in our modern world," Bo said. "It's like how the natives in Mexico used to grind food with pestle and mortar. None of the Mexican restaurants here use those tools anymore."

"Are we eating burritos?" Melvin plopped the shrimp down into his bowl.

"Lower your voice," Esther said.

Melvin lowered his voice. "I'm just saying that's a bad example. And misleading. Because no, we're not eating burritos, are we? Menudo? Chimichanga?"

"Stop it, Melvin."

"Tortas? Tostadas?"

"You're acting like a baby," Esther said.

"BECAUSE WE'RE NOT MEXICAN, ARE WE?"

Esther turned to Bo and spoke softly. "Why do you need to save time and energy?"

"I just want to save it."

"That's fine. But do you not have enough time and energy? Is there anything we can help with?"

"No."

"If you eat on a plate with silverware," Esther said, "it doesn't match with our utensils. Don't you want to match?" She wanted to end this argument now because if it didn't end here it'd continue at night, in bed, and the thing she treasured most after Bo, Larry, and Sonny was a good night's sleep of at least eight hours. In that exact order: Bo, Larry/Sonny, eight hours of sleep, Melvin, a filling meal.

"If you switch to plates and forks, you can match with me," Bo said.

"I have no problems with that," Esther said.

"We're not switching," Melvin said.

"Why do you dislike forks and spoons?" Bo asked.

"A fair question," Esther said.

"I don't dislike them," Melvin said. "They do their jobs competently."

"Americans use them," Bo said. "We're Americans."

"You're Chinese biologically and American politically," Melvin said, "because politically you were born here. So you take only the best of either culture, like chopsticks, and throw out the things that are only competent, like forks and spoons. Why do you think we speak two languages?"

"You use Cantonese to say curses you don't think I understand," Bo said.

"I curse in both languages," Melvin said.

"No cursing here," Esther said.

"I'm just saying if I wanted to, I can curse in either language," Melvin said. "The Chinese have used chopsticks for thousands

35

of years. What's wrong with using something our ancestors created?"

"Maybe our ancestors also created forks and spoons," Bo said.

Esther smiled and noticed Melvin noticing her smile, which made her smile wider. What she enjoyed about arguments between Bo and Melvin was they allowed her to side with her son. She hoped he saw her as a loyal friend.

"Maybe our ancestors gave forks and spoons to Marco Polo," Bo said.

Melvin enjoyed spaghetti, and each time he ate it, made sure to note how it was a Chinese invention by way of Marco Polo. The history of spaghetti, like the history of many things in the world, was a Chinese one according to Melvin. "We gave them noodles," he often said, "and they threw tomato sauce and basil leaves on it. Strange, but works for me."

"Marco Polo?" Melvin asked, staring at Bo's plate.

Bo began eating.

Melvin's eyes were fixed on his plate.

"Stop staring," Esther said.

"Who are you?" he asked Bo finally. "Who are you?"

Sparking the Fire
(1976)

Today you are an American boy. Before long you will be an American man. It is important to America and to yourself that you become a citizen of fine character, physically strong, mentally awake, and morally straight.

Matches are OK for starting cooking fires. A campfire deserves better. Add to its romance by lighting it the way Indians and early settlers did it.

—*Official Boy Scout Handbook*

Against Esther's wishes, Melvin enlisted Bo in a Boy Scout troop headed by an old army friend. Even though Bo had never been a Cub Scout, the army friend agreed to allow him into his troop as a favor to Melvin. The army friend promised to teach Bo basic skills that would enable him to survive a week in the woods with only a knife, a mango, and a flashlight. He prescribed a diet filled with more steak and fish to boost Bo from a hundred pounds to at least one-thirty, and a weightlifting program to be implemented as soon as Melvin could get the money together and Esther gave him permission to buy a bench and a set of weights.

Esther refused permission and also refused to add more

steak and fish to the menu, so Melvin began cooking dinners that preceded the ones she prepared. Each night Bo had the option of choosing which dinner he wanted to eat. Each night he chose both, and ate half of what he'd normally eat from each sitting.

This frustrated Esther because Melvin's dinners mostly came out of a can or a box. Steak and fish he fried until "they were ready," readiness equaling a burnt black.

"He's a terrible cook," she said. "And why do you eat with a man who doesn't respect your choice of utensils? You don't have to eat both dinners. You can make a choice."

"It wouldn't be fair to the other person," Bo said.

Melvin's dinners began at six. Esther's began at seven. For two hours each night, the Lum kitchen was filled with the noise of clanging pots and pans, clanking dishes, and clacking chopsticks being washed, dried, washed again, and dried again.

This was just the beginning.

Melvin decided Bo had to learn to start a fire before his first Scout meeting. "A basic skill he needs to know."

"Are the other boys going to ask him to start a fire for them when they meet?" Esther asked. "Is he going to have to bring them the head of a deer, too?"

She thought Bo would refuse to go along with Melvin, and she was ready to support her son. "I can tell him you don't want to be a Scout. I can tell him for you."

"It's okay," Bo said.

"Why is it okay?"

"Because I don't think I've ever done anything to make him happy. I've only done things to upset him."

"You've gone back to chopsticks," she said.

"Yeah," Bo said. "Less efficient."

"If you do things to make me happy, that's more than enough," she said.

"I have to give it a try."

A week and a half before Bo's first meeting, Melvin came home with a duffel bag and a big smile on his face. From the bag, he pulled out a tan shirt. There was a Scout badge stitched on the left breast pocket.

"Put it on." He handed Bo the shirt. He pulled out a red neckerchief and wrapped it around Bo's neck. "Fits okay. You're lucky to be a Scout. When I was your age, we didn't have Boy Scouts. We had tongs. I stayed off the streets after six. At night, they ran around collecting protection money from businesses and rumbling with rival tongs.

"They stabbed each other with knives, beat each other on the head with bricks. My best friend Hung lost his right eye from a broken glass bottle in a rumble down in the Mission District."

"Sounds like a rough upbringing," Esther said.

Melvin ignored her.

"What was the name of the tong in your neighborhood?" Bo asked.

"The YMCA," Esther said. "By rumbling, he means the YMCA-sponsored track meets in Golden Gate Park."

Melvin glared at her. "Now you do everything your Scout leader tells you to," he said. "If he tells you to wrestle a mountain lion, you roll up your sleeves and take a deep breath."

"Why would there be mountain lions?" Esther asked.

"I'm telling him be prepared," Melvin said. "It's the Scout motto. You wouldn't know."

Esther was bothered by this scene of father standing over son, straightening his uniform, adjusting his neckerchief clasp, and picking lint off his shoulder.

Bo was her son, not his.

She flipped through the Scout book Melvin brought home and saw an illustration of boys crouching on all fours tracking rabbit prints in the snow. Another picture showed boys lying face down on a frozen lake, holding hands to form a human chain, pulling out someone who'd fallen in.

She understood why her husband would be so excited about involving her son in this business. Whereas common sense suggested that one avoid stepping on a frozen lake and following a rabbit in the snow, when there was no good reason to be on a frozen lake and no good reason to follow a rabbit unless you were going to kill it—in which case the sparse meat of a rabbit, especially in winter, did not justify the efforts of several hunters, much less one—Melvin lacked common sense and eschewed it in favor of doing things that made no sense.

What did Scout activities do but force boys to eat beans cooked in distant dirt holes (when nutritious tofu and rice were always available at home) and hunt little animals that possessed more bone than meat? Such pointless activities reminded her of the Chinese proverb about the man who was so useless he ate himself full of rice and couldn't even produce shit.

When Esther protested against Bo's involvement with the Boy Scouts, Melvin said, "I let you teach him how to cook."

"An omelet!" she said.

"I gave you that one, you give me this one."

"I've given you more than one," Esther said, remembering how Melvin had encouraged Sonny and Larry to take advantage of lonely widows, talking the boys up about the honor of finding food from outside the home, all that foolishness. It hadn't been until Larry's impending college graduation seven years ago that Melvin finally consented to side with her.

She'd told Larry that his uncle Phil knew a Dr. Nanda at UCSF who could write a note exempting him from the draft.

"Why?" Larry had asked. "If I get drafted, I get drafted."

"You can have a doctor's note," she said. "You know how many people your age would love to have this option?"

"What will it say?"

"You don't need to know," she said.

"I don't want a note saying I have one testicle or boils on my ass. I'm a healthy man, not a cripple."

"I don't care what you want. You're applying to dental school."

"Why?" Larry asked.

"Does every response have to be why? You don't have to challenge my every word. You can accept, once in a while, that I speak from a wiser and more knowledgeable perspective than you. Accept it. Stop asking why. Do what I say.

"Dental school because medical school would be too difficult for you and you're not clever enough for law school. Dental school because dentistry's a good, consistent paycheck. No matter what happens to the economy, there will always be jobs for doctors, dentists, and funeral directors. You wouldn't be happy working with dead people.

"And I'm complimenting you here, you have strong hands. A good dentist needs strong hands."

"No," Larry said.

"Do you have something against dentistry?" Esther asked. "Give me one good reason why you don't want to be a dentist."

"I can't think of one right now," Larry said. "Does Dr. Nanda even exist?"

"Of course," Esther said. "And so does the application. Come by tomorrow to pick it up. I've already typed most of it for you."

41

"Where am I applying?" Larry asked.

"UCLA."

"Why?"

She asked Sonny to talk to him.

"I tried," Sonny said.

"Did you really? Did you talk to him as if your own life depended on it?"

"I said, 'Hey man, if you got killed in Vietnam, I'd be really bummed out.'"

"Convincing." Esther then asked Melvin to talk to him.

"Maybe we should give him a choice," Melvin said.

Esther wanted to ask, You really want them to go through what you went through? She didn't know what he'd gone through in his war because he never talked about it. So she said, "Let me tell you what Larry is worth to me. He's worth the thirty-three hours I spent in labor when I screamed my throat sore. Remember? You plugged your ears with toilet paper. You had that luxury.

"I nursed that boy until my breasts about fell off. He left teeth marks across my shoulders. And to raise him just so he could say with your encouragement, 'Ah-Mah, I'm going out for candy.'"

Melvin nodded as she spoke. When she finished he said, "I'll tell him to take the note," and she realized that their marriage wasn't a complete disappointment. Faced with the possibility that Larry could get killed in battle, Melvin wanted an alternative, and that was a good enough reason for her to respect him.

Melvin invited Larry for lunch and a talk. He asked the boy to follow her plan.

"Dr. Nanda really agreed to write the note?" Larry asked.

"Of course." Esther showed him a copy of the typed letter. A smile crept onto his face as he read. "Tell him don't send it."

"Why?"

"I didn't get drafted," Larry said. "Sonny said you wouldn't actually go to the trouble of finding a real letter from a real doctor. We bet on it. Ten bucks. I was betting on you." He sounded as if she should take pride in his faith in her, which was worth no more than ten dollars!

She was furious. If she could've articulated complete sentences, she'd have said, Of course I would have found a letter for you. You're my son. You're also a gullible fool. Who do you think you are?

Melvin went to the garage and returned with a rolled-up newspaper.

"You really love me," Larry said to them. "Wow."

"Love. You?" was all she could manage before Melvin whacked Larry hard on the side of the head.

"Ow!"

"Get out!" Melvin smacked him on the head again and chased him out of the house. Esther would always be proud of her husband for this act. To her, it was one of his greatest moments.

They refused to see or talk to Sonny and Larry for three months, and when Larry decided to attend UCLA's School of Dentistry, she believed it was to pacify their anger.

In rare form, Sonny followed his older brother by enrolling in UCLA's M.B.A. program, which he dropped out of halfway through. Now twenty-six and employed at Wells Fargo, he visited on weekends to do his laundry and eat free meals. On discovering Bo's involvement with the Boy Scouts, he saluted him and asked, "What's the difference between a good log and a bad one? You prefer refried beans or green ones?"

Esther pulled Sonny into her room. "Say one more word to him," she said, "even look at him strangely and you'll be doing your laundry somewhere else."

"Jesus, Ah-Mah."

"Stop picking on him."

"Fine."

Bo's first fire-making lesson began with Melvin placing a piece of cloth at the end of a stick. He lit the cloth with a match and then tossed it into a coffee can to snuff out the flame. Bo watched silently.

"What are you doing?" Esther asked.

"Charring the cloth," Melvin said.

"Why?" she asked.

"It'll catch the sparks that Bo will make. It'll burn easier after it's charred."

"You just lit it with a match. If you didn't put out the fire, you would have fire."

"Yeah," he said.

"Can't Bo just light a match?" she asked.

Melvin ignored her. He handed Bo a piece of steel and a piece of flint. Then he draped the charred cloth over a collection of twigs and sticks arranged in a square in the middle of the concrete patio floor. "Strike the steel against the flint. Yes, down in that direction so the sparks fly onto the cloth."

"You just lit the cloth with a match," Esther said.

"Be quiet."

"You have many more matches."

"Go inside," Melvin said. "This is a private lesson."

"Bo wants me to stay," Esther said. She looked at the boy, who looked at the tools in his hands.

"Bo needs you to go inside," Melvin said.

"Bo, can I stay and watch?"

Bo nodded, then looked at Melvin, who shook his head.

"Nope," Melvin said.

"Bo said yes."

"Bo, tell her you can't light a fire with her watching you."

"I can."

"There," Esther said.

"No, you can't." Melvin growled.

"Ah-Mah, please go inside."

"I want to cheer you on."

"She wants to cheer me on," Bo said.

"You don't start a fire with someone cheering you on," Melvin said. "You do it because it means the difference between life and death, between surviving the night's cold or hypothermia."

"Then I might need to learn this survival skill, too," she said.

"Did I stand over your shoulder when you were teaching him how to make an omelet?" Melvin asked.

"I wouldn't have minded," she said. "You could have used the lesson."

"Go inside."

He and Bo waited. Bo looked nervous and Esther didn't want him to be. She wanted him to side with her without reluctance or fear. "You are more of a child than he is, Melvin." She went in and slammed the glass door shut.

They turned their backs to her and hunched together. Melvin began giving Bo instructions. His right hand wavered inches from his son's back, like he was a pastor giving his boy a benediction, blessing the sticks and praying for a good fire.

Bo began striking the steel against the flint.

Each night Esther watched as Melvin gathered tinder and kindling sticks and arranged them in a square crisscross, over

45

which he spread the cloth, freshly charred and ready to receive the sparks that would ignite the flames he longed to see.

For half an hour, Bo would scratch the flint with the steel, producing only a screeching sound that echoed the cries of the crickets who lived on the other side of the fence, and who were probably annoyed at the men trying to ruin their black night with heat and light.

Every five minutes, Bo put his tools down and Melvin helped stretch the boy's arms and back. Bo often asked Melvin about growing up in Hong Kong.

Melvin was seven when he moved to San Francisco with his parents, but he spoke of his birthplace with such vividness that one might have believed the man had spent a lifetime there. "The roaches in Kowloon are big as your forearm. They suck human blood."

"I don't think roaches suck blood," Bo said.

"Maybe, maybe not. But they were everywhere."

"What was the shopping like?"

"On the streets of Hong Kong, you can buy meatballs for lunch, get your shoes shined, and have a suit made. You can order a bowl of rice porridge at two in the morning. Shops and restaurants stay open through the night, which is perfect for a vampire like you."

"It'd be nice to visit," Bo said.

At session's end, he would watch quietly as Melvin gave the flint several hard strikes. The cloth would catch and a small flame flicker from the center of the stick pile.

Esther watched her son, dressed in his uniform, learning an obsolete skill. What were matches for? Lighters? Bo had been such an articulate proponent of efficiency and technological advance in his argument for the fork and spoon.

Two nights before his first Scout meeting, Bo had success.

"Come, flames!" Melvin shouted. He was crouched next to Bo and rocking on the balls of his feet.

Bo's head was bowed low, his back to her.

"There!"

She slid the glass door open. "Bo, you have homework."

"Quiet. He's almost got it."

She approached and walked around the stick pile to face them. Bo's neckerchief clasp glinted in the moonlight like one of Melvin's brass shell casings.

It started as a tiny spark, something one would have imagined harmless and incapable of producing anything. But it was the spark that caught, and Melvin and Bo whooped it into a small fire.

The twigs began to crackle.

Melvin and Bo didn't notice Esther as she went to pick up the garden hose behind them. They were slapping each other on the back when she turned on the spigot. They were fanning the flames when she approached. Only when they noticed her standing above them did she press the trigger and extinguish the fire with a powerful jet of water.

"What the hell are you doing?" Melvin asked.

But it'd already been done.

"Why did you do that?" Bo asked. "You shouldn't have done that." He looked at the soggy pile and then at her. Then he walked into the house.

Melvin stood. It was cold and dark. He nudged the wet sticks and they sloshed under his foot. "You could have let him enjoy it a little longer."

"You were enjoying it, too," she said.

"You could have let us enjoy it a bit more."

"It's not safe to have a fire burning in the middle of a patio."

Melvin exhaled. She could see his breath. "It's dangerous," she said. "He could have been burned."

Melvin chuckled. The chuckle extended into laughter and the laughter grew loud.

"Don't make fun of me," she said.

"Did you see the size of that fire?" Melvin asked. "It couldn't have burned a hair off my ass."

"Mr. War Hero doesn't care if he gets hurt, that's fine. I have to watch out for my son's safety."

"War hero was your idea," he said. "You're the one who kept telling the boys I shot Nazis and freed France."

"I wanted them to think well of their father."

"You don't care what they think of me. The worse the better."

Melvin's eagerness to leave for France had made her feel miserable and lonely after his departure, more so than if he'd left reluctantly. If he'd been mowing down Nazis with his machine gun, liberating villages, and feeding starving French children, she'd have understood why he left and she wouldn't have felt as if the time spent worrying for his life had been wasted.

"I handed out food to nobody," he said, picking his foot out of the wet stick pile. "I killed no one. I spent most of my time passing through wrecked towns and helping bury dead soldiers and civilians.

"The only person I shot was Jimmy Zahn, in a firefight. It was hell. The air was filled with dust. Couldn't see my hand in front of my face. I shot him in the thigh. Listened to his body hit the ground. His screams led me to him. I covered his mouth until it was over. Then I helped carry him to the medic, and for the rest of the war he didn't speak to me for shooting him."

Melvin once claimed to have met General Patton, a soft-spoken man who played a mean game of blackjack and who sang a rendition of "Danny Boy" that made him cry every time he replayed it in his mind.

She didn't know whether he got these details from bad war movies or bad war novels. He might have shot a friend who might have been named Jimmy Zahn, but she'd long since lost faith in what he said.

She'd always told their sons good stories about him. Stories about him passing out crackers and peanut butter to French children, and defending villages against German tanks with just his machine gun and a picture of her. He should have kept this story to himself.

If he wanted to disappoint her, she'd fire right back.

"When you were gone, I fell in love with Francis Saldovar," she said. "I visited his shop as much as possible, even on days I didn't need to buy meat. He smiled whenever I walked into his store. He touched my chest once." It'd been an accident. He'd slipped over a patch of lamb's blood and fallen on her, after which he apologized several dozen times.

"I remember him," Melvin said. "He died a few years ago. You flew back up to San Francisco for his funeral."

"Yes."

"I always thought it was strange for you to go to the funeral of an old butcher," Melvin said. "Was he a good butcher?"

"A great butcher and a wonderful man. He always gave me special discounts."

Melvin said nothing.

"Aren't you upset?" she asked.

He shook his head. "Francis was a good man. He probably would have been a better husband for you."

She went inside and shut the glass door behind her. She

watched him standing there in the patio, his back to her and his hands in his pockets, staring up at the sky.

She used to fantasize about marrying Francis because he was there, two blocks away, and she didn't know if Melvin would return. She'd imagined having children with Francis, boys and girls who'd wear aprons and stand on footstools to wrap meat for customers. He had simplified her idea of happiness, and made her believe kindness was a smile and affection thirty-five percent off tenderloin.

She went to check on Bo. His presence always comforted her. He was seated at his desk reading a chemistry book. He looked up.

"I'm sorry I put out the fire," she said. "I didn't know starting fires made you happy."

"You don't know what makes me happy," Bo said. "I don't know what makes you happy. I thought I knew what makes Ah-Bah happy, but starting a fire isn't enough to keep him happy."

"Then why did you do it?"

"Have you ever been to Hong Kong?" he asked.

"No," she said.

"I think it'd be a fun place to live."

"They were just stories, what he told you."

"He exaggerates," Bo said. "It's his way of joking."

"What would you do in Hong Kong?" she asked.

"Rent an apartment. Walk the streets. Ride the ferry. Talk to complete strangers."

"We have streets here."

"But no people on the streets," he said. "Our streets are made for cars, not walking. All the stores close before eight. Nothing stays open through the night."

"You don't have to leave this country to live in a big city."

"It was his city. I'd like to see where he came from."

"He came from his mother's body," she said.

He looked at her like she didn't know what she was talking about.

"You make me happy," she said.

"I'm your son. That's a matter of fact. I didn't do anything to make you happy."

"You don't have to do anything," she said.

"Making someone happy is labor. You earn someone's happiness. You have to work for it."

"That's not true," she said.

"Like me making an omelet the way you make it. Dice the tomatoes. Ditto the green peppers and mushrooms. Add pinchfuls of salt and pepper. Don't use handfuls, and don't just pour all over the place. You're not raining salt here. Pinchfuls." He was quoting her. Verbatim.

He sighed, like she did when she was frustrated with Sonny, Larry, and Melvin. "I haven't done a thing to make you happy," he said.

"Making someone happy isn't a job."

"You don't know what makes me happy," he said.

"Then tell me."

"I'm going to that first Scout meeting."

"That'll make you happy?"

"That'll make him less unhappy," Bo said. "I don't know what makes that man happy, either."

Deliverance at Yosemite
(1976)

A heat wave set in the second week of July, baking most of
Orange County in hundred-plus-degree weather. However, Bo
refused to come out of his locked room. Each evening he
remained inside, his electric fan set on high, the whir audible
through the door. Each evening Melvin was slumped on the sofa
in the living room, wearing just boxer shorts, his pale torso
reflecting the blue glow from the TV. Each evening Esther sat on
the patio fanning herself with the newspaper, hoping Bo would
come outside and chat with her.

Inside, Bo read history books detailing the rise and fall of
dynasties and empires, Asian and European. This wasn't required reading because he wasn't taking summer school. He was
reading for fun, and whenever she'd clean his room, she would
inevitably find a thick text bookmarked to a page recounting the
bloody crusades of twelfth-century English knights or the massive fleets of the Mongolian empire.

The first week of July Bo had reluctantly, and at Melvin's
request for brotherly bonding, followed Sonny and Larry to
Huntington Beach. There they threw Bo, against his permission,
into the ocean.

Bo had walked through the front door dripping wet and
mumbling curses at his brothers.

Sonny and Larry remained on the porch, apprehension on their faces as Esther demanded an explanation.

"The ocean's so big," Sonny explained, "and he's so small."

"It seemed like fun at the time," Larry said. "He was shouting."

"He was probably shouting for you to put him down."

"They could have been shouts of joy and anticipation," Sonny said.

"You're terrible brothers," she said.

Their hands were stuffed in the pockets of their shorts.

"Irresponsible. Disloyal. Uncaring."

Melvin came up from behind her. "You two want to come in?"

She turned and glared at him.

"Maybe not," Melvin said.

"Yeah," Sonny said. "We should get going."

She slammed the door shut as Sonny and Larry walked back to Sonny's car. "Your idea," she said to Melvin.

"Give them time to sort it out themselves," he said. "Brothers do this sort of thing to each other."

"What if he drowned?"

"They wouldn't have let him drown," he said.

"Your fault." She went to Bo's door and knocked. The fan was whirring loudly inside the room. "Bo."

"I'm busy."

"What're you doing?"

"Drying off."

"I scolded your brothers."

He opened the door, standing in a dry pair of shorts and a dry white T-shirt. His wet clothes were draped over the back of his chair, which was positioned right in front of the whirring fan. "You shouldn't have."

"I thought I should say something," she said.

"It's none of your business," he said, frustration in his voice. "Leave it alone."

"Leave what alone?"

"My brothers and I." Bo ran a hand through his wet hair. "It's our business."

"They were wrong," she repeated.

"I know. I was there."

"I'm just trying to help."

"I don't need it."

"Okay," she said.

"Okay," he said. Then he shut the door.

She stood waiting for him to open it again, but he didn't. Finally she turned and walked back out to the living room.

The price tag initially intimidated Esther. In addition, Christmas was five months away and Bo's birthday had been a month prior. After staring at it through the Sears display window for half an hour, she made her decision. She really had no excuse, but in the hope of gaining her son's affection, she was willing to pay the price.

When Melvin saw it, he asked, "You know how much two hundred fifty dollars is?"

"Two hundred fifty dollars."

"For some fancy useless machine," he said.

"It's a gift."

"When's the last time you spent this much money on Sonny or Larry?"

Esther didn't answer.

"When's the last time you bought them a gift for no reason?" he asked.

"They have Helen and Mirla to buy them gifts."

Melvin shook his head, let out a long exasperated breath, and went to the bathroom.

When Bo saw it, he said nothing. He ran his hands over the box, looking at the sides and back. He picked it up and scoured every inch of the box's surface, his mouth open.

"A Marantz Superscope," he said finally. He cut open the box with a pair of scissors and lifted the machine out. "It's pretty heavy."

"But small and portable. You can carry it around with you when you want to go outside."

"Outside," he said, a look of wonder in his eyes.

In the following weeks Bo took his portable tape player with him wherever he went. It was, as Esther had said, small. But it was also, as Bo had said, heavy at about ten pounds, a gray steel box with tiny levers on the top and an ejectable cassette tray, into which Bo would slide blank tapes to record all the noises that filled his world. Afternoons he lugged it outside, sometimes with both hands. Nights, he lugged it back into his room.

Dinner for Melvin had always been a solemn activity reserved for eating and silence, but whenever Bo brought the Superscope to the dinner table, Melvin would speak to it like it was a child in need of amusement. While Esther and Bo were busy eating, Melvin would every now and then turn his head to the Superscope seated next to him and say things like "It's so hot I can fry noodles on my ass." Then he'd play back the recording and laugh. "Did you hear that?" he'd ask.

Bo brought it out to the front yard and let it record singing birds and passing traffic while he read his history books. For hours he would lay his head on a rolled-up sleeping bag and read or sleep while the Superscope recorded. Watching him next to the machine, Esther felt at peace, at least until Melvin decided to organize the first annual Lum weekend camping trip at Yosemite National Park (for the Lum men only).

Sonny had just proposed to Mirla, and Melvin wanted to get in one outing with his sons before Sonny was, in Melvin's words, whipped.

To Esther's surprise, Bo didn't resist the idea of the trip. "It's the last time we'll be together before Sonny gets whipped," he said.

Esther disliked Bo's use of Melvin's phrase. "You never spent time with your brothers before," she said.

"That's why this'll be the last time." There was again frustration in Bo's voice. He showed his impatience with her more these days. Whenever she'd stop by his room before going to bed, he'd look at the ceiling, look at the wall, look at his feet, yawn, and rub his eyes. He'd make every signal he could without actually saying the words, Please leave.

"You can bring the Superscope with you," she suggested. It was impractical to bring on a camping trip. It was too heavy, particularly if hiking was involved. Besides, would the machine even be capable of picking up any radio stations in the middle of the woods?

But it was her gift and she wanted it to go with him. Maybe he could record things Melvin, Sonny, and Larry didn't want her to hear, things that would give her a new perspective on these Lum men.

Bo looked at it. "I guess I can bring some music tapes. It'll kill time."

Thursday evening the men, dressed in khaki shorts, flannel shirts, and fishing hats, threw their sleeping bags and backpacks into Melvin's station wagon. Bo, in an oversized fishing vest and jeans, carried the Superscope with him into the backseat.

"We're off," Melvin said to Esther, who stood on the driveway looking at her sons in the car. "It's only a couple days."

"I know," she said.

"I'm surprised you didn't raise a fuss," he said.

"Bo wanted to go," she said. "What can I say?"

Melvin's lips began to curve upward; a victor's smug smile. She hated having to regard him as a competitor for Bo's affection.

"It's only a couple days," Esther said, then turned around.

"Aren't you going to kiss me good-bye?" Melvin asked as she walked back into the house and shut the door behind her.

Inside Esther grew nervous. Bo was now going to be alone with his brothers and Melvin for an entire weekend. What would become of him? What kind of pranks would they pull on her youngest son?

The men returned Sunday afternoon, their faces red with sunburn, and faint smiles all around. Esther felt like she'd missed a good party.

"You have fun?" she asked Melvin. He nodded, then walked into their bedroom and crashed onto their bed. Soon he was snoring into his dirt-covered fishing hat.

She took his hat off and tossed it in their bathroom sink.

She went to Bo's room and asked, "You have fun?"

He smiled and nodded, the pocket of his fishing vest stuffed with cassette tapes.

"Good," she said. She waited a moment while he stared at the Superscope on his desk.

"I'll let you get back to whatever you were doing." She turned and left the room, closing the door behind her.

The summer came to an end and soon school started. Bo entered his sophomore year of high school changed. He smiled more. He met friends. He didn't stay cooped up in his room all day and night, and though Esther knew she should be happy at this turn of events, she was afraid that he was changing too drastically, too quickly.

Bo was someone who used to lose sleep nights before his own birthday parties; he often requested the invitation list be trimmed down to just the immediate family, and the parties—quiet except for the clinks of glasses filled with soda and the slurps of men pigging out on cake and chips—felt more like wakes.

She had misjudged him, had missed the signs of his slow evolution from homebound introvert to personable, easygoing extrovert.

While cleaning his room one afternoon, she discovered the cassette tapes in his top desk drawer. They were marked by the dates of the weekend camping trip in Yosemite.

She put the first tape in the Superscope and pushed play. She would spend three afternoons listening while Bo was at school. Each time after she finished, she would rewind the tape completely, slip it back into its plastic case, and return it to the drawer.

July 23rd

"This is kind of like *Deliverance*," Larry said. He was breathing heavily. There were the sounds of dry twigs crackling, of heavy steps thudding. They were hiking.

"Like *Deliverance*?" Sonny said. "This is *Deliverance*. Four guys in the woods."

"What's this deliverance talk?" Melvin asked. "Is that something from the Bible?" He added with a laugh, "When did you guys turn Christian?"

"It's a book about four men who vacation in the woods," Larry said.

"Yeah, what happens?" Melvin asked.

"One of them gets ass-raped by a wild, hairy mountain man," Sonny said, then added, "Fuck," with shock and urgency in his voice, like it had actually happened to a friend of his.

A long pause. A crunch of dead leaves. An uneasy silence.

Bo hadn't spoken and Esther's heart froze with concern for her youngest son, who must at this point have been petrified.

"Let's get one thing straight," Melvin said. "This is a story. Right?"

"I don't think it's fiction," Sonny said.

"Yeah, I remember finding it in the nonfiction area of the library," Larry said.

"What were *you* doing in a library?" Melvin asked.

Larry didn't answer.

"Nobody's going to get ass-raped by a mountain man," Melvin said. "I didn't fight in World War II just to come home and get porked by some crazy bushman."

A burst of laughter from Sonny and Larry.

"What?" Melvin said.

"You said bushman," Sonny said.

"You don't have to worry, Ah-Bah," Larry said. "Bo's the pretty one here."

"Shut up," Bo said.

"You shut up," Larry said.

"Stop," Melvin said. "We're a family. We have to stick together."

"Good thing I brought this," Sonny said. There was the sound of a hand tapping something hard, and Esther knew it was Sonny's knife, a large, dangerous weapon he'd bought in Tijuana. "Nobody's porking me in the ass," he said with the reassurance of someone carrying a foot-long knife.

The sound of footsteps and heavy breathing resumed. Grunts every so often. The long march. Upward? Down a hill? It was hard to tell. The only sound Esther could clearly identify was that of exhaustion.

"That looks like a good spot," Melvin said. "You doing okay?"

"Yeah," Bo said.

"Watch your cornhole, Bo!" Sonny shouted, his voice distant. He and Larry had probably gone ahead.

"You want me to carry that?" Melvin asked.

"I'm all right," Bo said.

"It's too heavy."

"I'm fine," Bo said.

"He's fine," Esther said.

A pause.

"That's what I like about you," Melvin said. "You know that's heavy. I know that's heavy. But you haven't complained. Not one word."

"I'm too tired to complain," Bo said.

"Fair enough. Then keep up."

July 24th
The sound of leaves crackling, bushes rustling.

"We were supposed to get Bo," Larry whispered.

"You wouldn't have gotten me," Bo whispered back. Crickets were chirping in the background. There was the rush of water in the distance. They were near a river.

"Bo let us use the tape machine," Sonny whispered. "That's good enough. Ah-Bah's a better mark anyway."

"How long are we going to sit here?" Larry asked.

"Until he shows up," Sonny said. "And lower your voice."

"There he is!" Bo said, excitement in his voice.

"Quiet," Sonny said. "All of you, shut up."

There was now just the sound of crickets and the rushing stream. Then Larry began giggling, and soon he was joined by Bo.

"Quiet!" Sonny whispered firmly. "What's so funny? Where else do you expect the old man to take a piss?"

"Do it now," Larry said.

Then, in a scene Esther could clearly picture: Melvin having just urinated into the river, his shorts unzipped and his sons huddled in bushes nearby under cover of darkness, and Sonny shouting in a low, Southern-accented voice, "Bend over, purty boy!"

"What?" Melvin answered, his voice small and uncertain, with a slight fear that brought a smile to Esther's face as she listened.

Melvin must have instantly zipped his shorts back up because Sonny shouted again in his accented voice, "Take them shorts off!"

"Who's there?" Melvin asked. "What do you want?"

"Take them off, you hairy monkey!"

"Sonny?" Melvin asked.

"Let's go," Larry whispered.

"Wait," Bo whispered back. The firmness in his voice struck Esther, the fact that he was telling his oldest brother what to do, the fact that Bo, in a day, had gone from potential victim to accomplice, having been successfully initiated into his brothers' confidence.

There was a moment of excitement as the boys nervously tittered and bumped each other. "Don't mess with me!" Melvin said. "I'm a veteran! I've been in combat."

The boys erupted into laughter.

"Sonny," Melvin's voice boomed from the distance, "you better run!"

"Let's go," Sonny said. "Bo, give me the tape deck."

"Come on!" Larry shouted.

"I'm going to kick your ass!" Melvin shouted, his voice louder now than it was before.

"It's too heavy for you," Sonny said, "and we've got to go."

"Here."

There was no resistance on Bo's part. He simply gave it up. No cajoling needed. No hesitation.

She listened to her sons' escape, to the sound of rustling bushes and crackling leaves, of wild shouts, flight, and laughter.

July 25th

The sound of Melvin's buzz-saw snoring, of a sleeping bag being unzipped.

"Hey, where are you going?" Sonny whispered.

"Out for a walk," Bo said.

"It's pitch black."

"I have a flashlight."

"Go back to sleep and shut up," Larry mumbled.

The sound of Bo's walking, the sound of Melvin's snoring getting smaller. Crickets chirping loudly now. The sigh of tree leaves bothered by a breeze.

"Wait up," Sonny said.

The rush of a river growing louder.

"Watch yourself," Sonny said. "If you fall, I'm not coming in to get you."

"I want to be alone," Bo said.

"You're always alone. Why don't you try being with people for once?"

Bo didn't answer.

"Why don't you like us?" Sonny asked.

"Of course I like you," Bo said. "You're my family."

"You treat us like we're in the way, usually in the way to your room."

"You guys are always at each other's throats," Bo said.

"I get along with Ah-Bah," Sonny said.

"Every time you come over, either you or Larry end up doing or saying something to make Ah-Mah angry. Then she starts yelling. Then Ah-Bah starts yelling at her to stop yelling. Then you and Larry are yelling back." He paused. "It's quieter in my room."

"We're brothers," Sonny said.

"Just because I don't follow you everywhere like Larry—"

"Larry doesn't follow me everywhere," Sonny said.

"He's your yes-man."

"He's loyal."

"Like a German shepherd," Bo said.

"What's your problem?"

"I wanted to be alone."

"We're in the middle of the woods," Sonny said. "It's pitch black. There's nobody around. What if you fell in the river?"

"I can swim."

A pause.

"Hey."

"Relax," Sonny said. "What do you think, I'm following you

just so I can push you in with that machine? I want to sit. I'm tired."

A long pause.

Some twigs snapped. Was Sonny just realizing that the Superscope was recording? Did he care?

"Why'd you bring that, anyway?" Sonny asked. "You should have left it at home."

"It made Ah-Mah happy for me to take it along."

"It's too heavy," Sonny said.

"Yeah."

"That's what you get for being her favorite," Sonny said, and Esther detected a hint of bitterness in his voice.

"You don't have to listen to her complain about Ah-Bah," Bo said. "Every night."

"Why do you think Larry and I used to get out of the house as much as possible?"

"I want to go somewhere," Bo said.

"TJ?" Sonny asked.

"Hong Kong."

"What are you going to do in Hong Kong?"

"I don't know," Bo said. "Ah-Bah made it sound like a fun place to live."

"Kind of far, don't you think?"

"You'd miss me?" Bo asked.

"Ah-Mah would. A lot."

"You don't know how hard it is. I'm cramming for a math exam and she's moaning about Ah-Bah walking around in his underwear."

Esther made a mental note: Don't complain about Melvin to Bo. But maybe she'd already made herself too much of a burden on him, made herself irrevocably an obstacle in his path, as

Sonny had said. And worst of all, it was Melvin who'd planted the seed in Bo, filling his head with visions of Hong Kong, of all places. That overcrowded shopping mall of a city.

"After I graduate from college, I'm going to leave," Bo said. "If she wants to call, she'll have to complain long distance and pay for it."

"You're only fifteen," Sonny said.

"And?"

"I guess it's okay to plan eight years ahead."

"You're going to stay in Orange County?" Bo asked.

"Mirla likes it here," Sonny said. "Besides, after you leave, someone will have to make sure Ah-Mah doesn't kill herself."

"She won't kill herself."

"No," Sonny said, "but she's not going to be happy when she hears this."

Good Form
(1989-2002)

After Bo moved to Hong Kong in 1989, Esther thought he'd feel the same way she did when he read her letters, that despite the passing of friends and lovers, they would each remain the most important person to the other.

She wrote about afternoons gardening and weekends playing mah-jongg with friends in Chinatown. She had the postman take pictures of her every few weeks. She didn't need him to remember her as a younger woman with fewer wrinkles or gray hairs. She wanted him to see her as she was in the here and now.

Bo wrote about his travels in Hong Kong, sightseeing from atop Victoria Peak, watching the waves from the deck of a harbor ferry, shopping in the various clothing and grocery districts in Kowloon.

He included photos of concrete skyscrapers cascading down the sides of green hills, fishermen selling the day's catch in makeshift booths of tarp and wood, children hawking Gucci and Christian Dior handbags in alleyways.

"I bought some pork buns from a street vendor and saw a Mel Gibson movie," he wrote.

"There's a place here with incredible chicken feet. I can suck on them all day.

"I've been writing Louis. He's a good kid. Of my nephews, he's the one I like best."

"You're right. He's the only nephew who writes me, but I still like him better than the other ones."

After he met Julie, he began sending photos of her, and the I changed to We. "We went sightseeing at Victoria Peak. We saw a movie. We ate chicken feet."

It broke Esther's heart. She wanted him to remain happily alone, to feel as completely fulfilled from receiving her letters as she felt from receiving his.

After Julie died in '93 from cancer, Bo stopped answering his phone and writing.

"How do I know if you're sick or not?" she wrote. "Or if you have any money? Can you let me know you're alive and in good health? Tell me you plan to keep on living. I'll come visit if you don't respond."

It surprised her that Julie's death had affected him so much, and she wondered if her own could affect him even more. She wrote of pains and aches she didn't have, but which her mah-jongg friends had talked about. She described arthritis and the occasional tightness in the chest, which she'd heard was like a fist squeezing the heart, and which wasn't actually a tightness so much as it was a pain that made it hurt to breathe. "But don't worry," she wrote Bo. "The pain is very, very severe no more than four times a week. I truly enjoy my new walking cane. It's polished oak."

He wrote back, "Ah-Mah, no need to visit. I'm fine, but I'm worried about your health. I asked Sonny to take you to a doctor. I hope you feel better."

"I don't believe you're fine," she wrote. "Write me more like you used to. I can buy an airplane ticket anytime. I can be there in a couple days. I can't believe you told Sonny."

"You're not well enough to travel," he wrote. "I'm fine. Here. I'm writing more. Like here. Right now. More."

To make matters worse, Sonny arrived one afternoon to take her to a doctor. "You're getting a checkup," he said.

"Nothing's wrong with me," she said, and Sonny talked about her symptoms, the list of pains she'd given Bo, all the aches her youngest son should have kept to himself.

"I thought you got a new walking cane," Sonny said.

"Why would I need a cane? Go home." She wanted Bo to write more, but she didn't want to anger him by being a continual nag. She would respect his privacy, but he needed to keep her updated on how he was doing. She created a form and sent it each month with a self-addressed stamped envelope. He wouldn't have to write. Wouldn't even have to pay for postage. All he'd have to do was check the boxes. If the most she could have was a set of X's marked in his ink, she would take it.

She wrote, "I know you're not in the mood to write, but please fill this out:"

Dear Son,	Yes	No
1) Are you sick?		
2) Are you sleeping at least seven hours a night?		
3) Do you have a job?		
4) Do you have a place to live?		
5) Should I send money?		
6) Do you always plan on waking up the next day?		

A good response was:

Dear Son,	Yes	No
1) Are you sick?		X
2) Are you sleeping at least seven hours a night?	X	
3) Do you have a job?	X	
4) Do you have a place to live?	X	
5) Should I send money?		X
6) Do you always plan on waking up the next day?	X	

Bo answered her forms for eight years. He always sent a good response and she believed he'd continue doing so until he stopped.

The U.S. and Hong Kong post offices had never mishandled a single exchange between her and her son, and Bo had always been prompt in returning the forms.

She sent an additional form every three weeks and waited for his reply. Given mail delay or delay on Bo's part, a response should still have arrived already. She waited five months before phoning him, which he'd made her promise never to do.

"*Wei?*"

"I'm calling for my son Bo," Esther said in Cantonese. "Can I talk to him?"

"I'm sorry. He moved out."

"Where?"

"He told me not to give out any information, especially to his mother or family."

Esther felt a bit of satisfaction in the fact that Bo had distinguished her from the rest of the family. "I have a right to know. Are you a mother?"

"I have a son."

"As a mother, you have a responsibility to tell me where he is."

69

"He made me promise not to tell," the woman said.

"I'm worried sick."

"I'm sorry."

"Tell me."

"He's alive and in good health. I know this for a fact, so please don't worry."

"I need to talk to him," Esther said.

The woman didn't respond.

"You're a cold-hearted dog!" Esther shouted.

When it began she thought an illness was surfacing and clouding her vision. The tears fell down her face faster than she could wipe away with her hand. Images she'd repressed now crystallized and she began sobbing for Bo, who in that moment was dead, his body crushed under an overturned taxi, his throat slashed by a mugger, his bones shattered from a leap off a skyscraper.

Who was this woman to tell her Bo was alive and in good health? For all Esther knew, this woman wasn't even a woman, much less a mother, but a man squeezing his vocal cords to squeak out a high voice.

Where had he gone? Did he kill himself? Why did he kill himself for Julie when his mother was alive and worth writing to?

Esther cried and the woman said nothing. She forced herself to quiet down. She sat up straight. She would not present herself badly, sniffling like a little girl. She held the phone away from her face and resurrected Bo. She imagined him slowly sitting up from the sidewalk he'd fallen onto. She saw the slit in his throat close together perfectly, leaving no scar. She saw the taxi flip back upright. Her son rubbed his head, stood, and walked away from the crash.

"Who the hell are you?" she asked.

"I was his landlady, and I'm very sorry."

Esther called Helen and Mick and told them to come to her house the next morning. She called Sonny and Louis, and neither of them answered. She left messages.

She couldn't sleep that night. She lay awake wondering where Bo had gone. She should have told him the one thing she'd never tell anyone else, that she prized him above his brothers and father. He had no right to disappear on her.

Hours passed on her alarm clock. She listened to the crickets until they got tired and stopped chirping.

She stared at the ceiling and wished Bo good health wherever he was. She wished him delicious meals, a firm bed, and warm blankets. She tried to remember all she could see, hear, and touch of him. Everything her memory would allow.

Lucky Boy
(1988)

The summer Louis's parents decided to vacation in Montreal was the summer he'd been planning to learn nine thousand new words so he could go guns blazing in his school's next spelling bee.

His father, Sonny, had just received a raise that afforded them five days in an exotic, but not too exotic, locale. Louis overheard the travel plans through their bedroom door.

"Paris?" his father asked. "We don't have enough money for Paris."

"Boston's exotic?" his mother asked.

"What about Tijuana?"

There was silence that must have been initiated by his mother's stare of rebuke, given out for C grades and incorrect travel suggestions.

"Toronto?" his father asked softly.

"Same continent," his mother said.

"They speak French in Montreal, Mirla."

There was a long pause before his mother said, "Fine," with a note of disappointment in her voice.

She came out and broke the news to him.

"Can't you leave me here?" he asked. He'd typed a schedule for the coming months and didn't want to sacrifice five days that could be used to memorize words De through Eg.

"Do you have any idea how fortunate you are to have parents willing to take you to a foreign country?" she asked. "When I was your age, I got weekend trips to the Garden Grove Sears."

She was not interested in his quest to take the school spelling title from Jason Hahn, the defending champion. She felt that because geography was the only subject he was getting C's in, geography was what he should be focusing on. Her disappointment only encouraged him not to focus on geography.

Learning to spell correctly was a righteous undertaking to Louis. A word could have various meanings, alternative pronunciations, a language of origin, and an etymology. An entire history behind each combination of letters.

Why waste time memorizing cities and countries? That's what atlases were for. Words were more interesting. Like the word cleave, which meant either adhering to or dividing. It had opposite meanings, which Jason Hahn couldn't fathom when he said, "Louis, you can't say, 'The baby panda cleaved to his mother.' You can't use cleaved that way." What good was knowing how to spell a word without knowing the meaning(s)? That was morally irresponsible and proved that Jason did not deserve the spelling title.

"I'll bring my word lists with me," Louis said to his mother.

"This is a vacation," she said. "None of us is bringing any work. No studying. Why are you so obsessed with the spelling bee? How is knowing how to spell loquacious going to help you in life? Why do you think we keep a dictionary in the house?"

"Because you and Dad can't spell."

"Do you even know where Montreal is?"

"Of course," Louis said even though he had no idea. "It's directly north of us."

"So if I draw a line that runs straight from Orange County up through Canada, I'll pass Montreal?"

He nodded and waited for her to tell him he was wrong. When she didn't, he felt a swell of pride. He smiled, expecting her to apologize for underestimating his knowledge of Canadian cities. "I'm exactly right, of course."

"Of course," she said.

"It's wonderful how we're flying a straight line north from southern California," his mother said, not looking up from her in-flight shopping catalog. Louis sat between her and his father, who was snoring softly, his head pressed against the window as if he was looking out at the white clouds below them that dotted the blue sky.

Before they'd taken off, his mother had asked a stewardess to show him their route. The stewardess had pulled out a map of North America and drawn with her finger a line that ran northeast from the red dot of Los Angeles to a red dot on the other side of the continent.

Louis ignored his mother and she continued flipping through the catalog.

When the stewardess came by with the beverage cart, he refused his peanuts and soda. "I'm fasting until I return to my country," he said. "And definitely no legumes. L-e-g-u-m-e-s. Legumes."

His mother closed the catalog and set it on her lap. She folded down her tray table and requested an orange soda and a bag of peanuts. Then she looked at him. "You might not appreciate this trip now. But I want you to know you are a very lucky boy.

When you're older, you'll look back on this day and realize how ungrateful you've acted toward me.

"When you were born, your grandmother wanted to have you. She wanted a baby around her house. She wanted to raise another child. She said to me, 'I would give anything to have Louis.'"

The stewardess handed his mother her food and drink, and rolled on.

The bag crunched as his mother opened it. She dropped two nuts in her mouth, chewed, and wiped her lips with a napkin, clearing away grains of salt.

"What a fatuous request," he said. "Fatuous. F-a-t-u—"

"We thought about it. We were looking for a new house. We could have used an extra ten thousand dollars, no questions asked."

"You thought about it?"

"Three days later, I told her we decided to keep you. She was heartbroken." His mother sighed wistfully as if she was remembering a handsome ex-boyfriend or a lunch that had hit just the right spot.

"We could have given you to her," his mother said. She sipped from her plastic cup. She chewed on another peanut. "Imagine that. A sixteen-year-old going out on dates, bringing girls home to meet his grandmother. You could have spent your youth buying denture cream and Metamucil, learning CPR, squeezing her nose at night to make sure she was still breathing. Like living with Miss Havisham."

"Miss Havisham?" Louis asked.

"A woman with money. You'll read about her in high school." His mother picked the catalog up off her lap and began searching for the page she'd been studying. She found it and whistled at a redwood wine rack with gold trim. "Well. Aren't you glad we decided to keep you?"

It happened in room 204 of the Port Royale Hotel in Montreal.

After a day of walking through Montreal's downtown, a day of Louis's father asking the natives for directions in slow English, these French speakers who also spoke perfect English and didn't need slow-pitch softball, after a day of marveling at *Stationment* signs that denoted the exotica of parking lots, and after a day of wandering the stately stoned walkways and soft green mounds of McGill University, the "Harvard of Canada," the university attended by William Shatner, Burt Bacharach, and most important to Louis's father, James Naismith, the Inventor of Basketball, and therefore the Father of the Greatest Sport on Earth, they arrived back at room 204, where Louis's parents, sweaty and tired from the day's trek, went to the bathroom to freshen up. They didn't lock the door.

Louis turned on the TV and sat at the foot of his bed. Brown bags and suitcases lay on the floor around him. He kicked the shoulder straps of his backpack while the weather reporter forecasted continuing high pressure and heat for the coming week.

"Why don't they say that Harvard is the McGill of the U.S.?" Louis heard his father ask. "Why is it when something's good in some foreign country, it's the Harvard of that country?"

"Nobody except Wes calls McGill the Harvard of Canada," his mother said, turning on the bath. "That's because he graduated from there."

Wes was one of his father's coworkers, but Louis didn't care about Wes or McGill. He needed to pee. He heard his parents giggling, the sound of water splashing that heightened the pressure in his groin. His parents were probably joking around, throwing water on each other. He heard his mother ask, "Sonny, is that your horn of plenty?"

"Oh, Mirla."

Louis, nine years old, had no idea what that meant. He forgot to knock. They'd only been inside a few minutes and he assumed their clothes would still be on as he opened the door.

He had seen his father's chest many times before, out in the yard or around the house on a hot day. It was nothing spectacular. His father had a pale, almost pink hairless torso that resembled an uncooked salmon steak, but his mother's breasts shocked him in the same way that Grendel's mother, as portrayed in the comic book series *Beowulf: Bloodstained Days*, had sent a shiver down to the core of his heart. Louis had always considered his mother a beautiful woman, but her nakedness shamed him and seemed monstrous in a way her fully clothed self never had.

He turned his eyes away from her body, thank god her lower half had been shielded by the side of the tub, and said, "Shit!" to which his father said, "Jesus!" to which his mother said, "Shut the door!"

He felt like a drunken Dane stumbling through the mead-hall, dazed, not sure where he was, and looking for Unferth and other comrades who weren't there. He shut the bathroom door, ran out of the hotel room, and sped down the gray carpeted hallway toward the elevator.

In the following weeks, he tried not to visualize his mother's breasts, but his effort to forget only crystallized the picture, the way the word Beelzebub sounded repeatedly in his head after he'd heard Pastor Elkin's sermon on keeping Satan out of one's thoughts.

In reflection years later, he would feel he'd judged her too harshly. He believed she'd been beautiful sitting there in the tub. He was certain she had not resembled Grendel's mother, whose spine bore a ridge of bony plates, whose forearms were covered with shaggy hair, whose breasts sagged, and whose nipples pointed forward like arrowheads.

He could have told his mother she didn't look gross or monstrous, but those words didn't sound comforting, so he never spoke them. He could have said other words to make sure she knew he thought she was fine and normal looking, but for weeks after the incident they said nothing, and he treated her like she was physically repulsive, flinching back unconsciously if she reached out to hand him something, stealing glances at her during dinner until she said, "Stop that. What's wrong with you?" after which she'd continue eating with a confused and sometimes pained look in her eyes.

The incident in the hotel bathroom remained a constant prick in his memory, haunting him in the most unexpected moments: while he showered or as he tried to fall asleep, treading that line between consciousness and dreams.

It was a simple gesture. His father was reaching for his mother's breasts with the eagerness of a child about to pick pears off a tree, and slathered on the old man's face was the biggest, strangest smile Louis had ever seen.

The Impossibility of Two Trains Colliding at One Hundred Miles Per Hour (1968)

Sonny accidentally scorched a section of Teresa Ribisi's shoulder-length hair while lighting a Bunsen burner in chemistry class. This prompted Mr. Ribisi to demand that Sonny shave his head as payment for Teresa's suffering, which had arrived in the form of a barber shearing away four inches of burnt hair.

Sonny asked his girlfriend what he should do. "Don't shave your head," Mirla said. "It was an accident."

The following night, Sonny visited Mr. Ribisi and handed him a paper sack filled with his black hair.

Mirla was not happy. "I owed the man," Sonny told her.

"Why didn't you tell me you were going to do it?" She ran her hands slowly over his scalp. He liked her fingertips gliding across his skin. He liked anything that had to do with her touching him.

When Mirla's father saw Sonny's head, he said, "I admire what you did for Mr. Ribisi. Brave of a young man to go slick." Mr. Ho ran his hands over the top of his own head, a gleaming dome traversed by a few strands of a comb-over. "But there are advantages to going goose egg, you know?"

Sonny didn't think there were advantages to being bald. He looked forward to his hair growing back, but he was happy the man he considered his future father-in-law admired what he had done.

The next day Mirla said they should break up.

"We'll be apart next year anyway," she said.

"Orange Coast is half an hour from UCLA," he said.

"I need to see more of life," she said. "I've never truly felt alive."

"Is it the hair? It'll grow back."

I've never felt truly alive? He knew what it was to feel alive, and it wasn't an abstraction, another way of saying, I don't know what I'm saying.

Life to Sonny had always been a series of pleasant tactile sensations. The relief in his belly after a satisfying, butt-numbing session on the toilet, the adrenaline high after an hour of pedaling a bike, her tongue against his cheek.

He begged her to change her mind. They were in her kitchen when she proposed the math exam. If he scored ninety percent or better, she'd stay with him. If not, they were done.

"Why are you doing this?" he asked.

She glared at the top of his head.

He waited for an answer.

She continued glaring at the top of his head.

He stood and looked out the sliding glass door. He stared at the bike in the far corner of the yard, at the streamers dangling like hair from the handlebars, at the curved outline of its sloping frame, at the rear wheel raised up in the air. From this distance, it looked like a bucking stallion frozen in mid-buck.

Mr. Ho had bought a Sears Spaceliner for Mirla's fourteenth birthday. She rode it for a few weeks before giving it up to devote more time to her studies. "Schoolwork!" Mr. Ho had said. "There are more important things to do." When he asked her to get back on the bike, she explained that the sidewalks had become too dangerous for riding. "Pigeons and kids everywhere."

In response, he nailed two blocks of wood close together and wedged the front wheel in between, fixing it in place. Then he ran several steel wires from the horizontal post of the yard fence to the bike's rear carrier, pulling up the bike's back end, suspending the rear wheel so Mirla could pedal continuously without moving an inch.

She rode it for a few days before saying that the seat made her butt sore, and the bike stayed untouched in the back of the yard until Sonny found it next to the clothes line on which were hung the wet, dripping socks and underwear of the Ho family. It was coated in cobwebs, and the frame, formerly hot pink, had rusted to a deep shade of brown.

He cleaned it, lubed the chain, and began riding an hour each night five nights a week while her parents read the newspaper in the living room.

"That thing cost me a fortune," Mr. Ho said. "Ride hard. Ride it until it breaks."

Riding a bike had always made Sonny happy, the feeling of his legs pumping and his heart beating rapidly, assurances that he was truly alive.

He slid open the door.

"Where are you going?" she asked.

"For a ride." He walked out to the bike and got on it. He started pedaling.

Mirla followed. She stood next to him, frowning. "You have two weeks to prepare. I'll let you write formulas on a notecard. One side only."

She explained what the exam would cover, and he thought

about the things they still had to do. They needed to get married. Then a honeymoon in Houston, where they could watch a rodeo. He had sharply defined quadriceps, powerful lungs, and a strong heart. He was chocolate ice cream. How could she not love chocolate ice cream?

But math was hard. At seventeen, his grasp of first order differential equations was tenuous. Linear equations of higher order baffled him. He had no hope with power series solutions, and no chance in hell with Fourier Series and separation of variables. This wasn't even high school math. This was Mirla math.

At seventeen, Mirla "The Human Abacus" Ho of Garden Grove High School was already a campus celebrity for having won the state Mathletics competition three times, appearing each year in the local section of the Orange County newspaper that'd given her the nickname.

Mirla was one of two Chinese students at Garden Grove High, and the *Register* had written, "Chinese high school student wins state math competition with help from oriental genes." Sonny had always hated her nickname because it made no sense. An abacus wasn't human. Mirla, as far as he knew, had never even touched an abacus. And oriental genes had shit to do with anything. He was Chinese, and math was a foreign language he couldn't speak.

"Are you listening?" Mirla asked.

He nodded and wiped sweat from his forehead, the rear wheel whirring behind him.

"What did I say about the exam?"

"It's going to be hard," he said.

"Then you should consider going home now."

"Why?"

"You've got a lot of studying to do," she said.

He pedaled harder.

"Suit yourself." She turned and walked back inside without saying another word.

The exam began at noon in her kitchen. Saturday. Her parents were visiting her grandparents. Though he was gone, Mr. Ho had remembered to leave Sonny a batch of freshly baked butter cookies to keep his strength up during the test. He'd also left a note that read, "Good luck, Sonny. Don't let her intimidate you."

She sat across the table from him. He smiled at her. She smiled back, looked over his head at the clock behind him, and said, "You may begin."

Problem number one:

1) A motor scooter starts from rest $(x_0 = v_0 = 0)$. It moves at a constant acceleration of 9 ft/s^2. Air + road resistance causes a deceleration of 0.5 ft/s^2 for every foot/second of the scooter's velocity v. (a) Work out a first order differential equation for $v(t)$. (b) Find v when $t = 15$ s. (c) Find the limiting velocity as t approaches $+ \infty$.

Sonny's answer:

(a) Who's riding the scooter? (b) Why not drive a car? (c) Why does there need to be air and road resistance? Why does there need to be a scooter?

He flipped through the exam. All the problems had been neatly typed. The rest of the questions were as hard as, if not harder than, the first one.

"If the max speed of two trains is one hundred miles per hour, they wouldn't collide head-on at that speed," he wrote. "They'd hit their brakes and try to stop. They'd collide at less than a hundred.

"Nobody can throw a baseball faster than two hundred fifty miles per hour. Maybe a very strong Martian, but not a human being.

"How could a rabbit, lion, and man race together on a track? How would you keep the animals in their lanes? Rabbits are wild creatures."

He ate a cookie, then another. "Have some. They're good."

She glanced at the clock behind him. "You still have a lot of problems left. You won't have much time to check your calculations."

He looked out at the yard. "It's a warm day. We should be outside."

She used to stand by him as he rode her bike because she enjoyed watching the rivulets of sweat run down his face. "They're like tears," she'd say, tracing the path the drops took from his forehead down to the corners of his eyes and farther down to the edges of his lips. "It's like you're crying."

"You like seeing me cry?"

"I imagine I just got run over by a car or hit in the head with a brick, and you're grieving. It makes me happy to know you could care so much for me."

He'd spin fast right from the start of each session. He didn't have time for a warmup. Didn't need one. When his face strained, when the sweat beaded on his forearms and soaked his shirt and shorts, she'd stop watching. She'd move up close. He'd push even harder and she'd run her tongue across his forehead and down his cheek.

He'd had to work for these kisses, for the smooth warmth of her tongue cleaning his face. He'd had to work until his heart began punching his chest, sweat dripped off his chin, and his mouth hung open in exhaustion, sucking air that filled his lungs and pushed the heart that punched his chest.

It was what Ah-Bah had said. Actually, it was what Ah-Bah had meant. His father had said the higher the monkey climbs up the tree, the sweeter the grapes it retrieves. Grapes didn't grow from trees, but Sonny had found the sweetness of labor to be true.

His make-out sessions with Mirla away from the bike had lacked excitement and danger. Any chump could make out with his girlfriend in the safe confines of a plush carpeted bedroom. It was when he rode almost to the point of passing out that he felt most like a Spanish conquistador who'd trekked several thousand miles to discover the New World's gold on behalf of Queen Isabella. And Mirla licking him was like the queen come down from her throne to personally thank him for finding all this gold. Any chump could be kissed by his lady, but the kiss always felt twice as good after an hour on the bike.

The riding provided other benefits. He'd been a chubby kid, and a year on the bike had burned twenty-five pounds off his body, which was now slim and hard. He was addicted to the workouts. If he missed a night, he'd feel anxious and jittery and wouldn't be able to sleep. He took the weekends off, and by Sunday night he couldn't wait to get back on the bike. Sunday nights he was doing squats in his garage and admiring his flat stomach in the bathroom mirror.

"You're not taking this test seriously," she said. "Stop daydreaming."

"I've been up studying the last three nights." He stood and

stretched his legs. They were stiff from all this sitting. He slid open the glass door and breathed the fresh, warm air outside.

"You're not even trying," she said.

"Doll, you don't even know." It was the first time he called her doll, and saying it made him feel like more of a man, like his body had just erupted with muscles, like his balls had just grown to the size of grapefruits.

"What did you call me?"

"Nothing." He sat back down and wrote answers for the rest of the problems. Seconds ticked away on the clock. Minutes passed. "Time's up," she said.

"You don't need to grade this." He returned to the front page of the exam, wrote his name on it, and slid it across the table to her.

"Why?" she asked.

"I didn't get a single one right."

"How do you know?"

"I'm sure. Don't break up with me."

She didn't respond. She looked at the front page, studied his answers, then shook her head. "First one's the easiest," she said.

"You haven't given me one good reason. If it's because I shaved my head, that's not a good reason." He waited for her to respond. She remained quiet, looking down at the test.

He stood and walked out to the bike. He got on and pedaled, beginning with a slow cadence.

She watched him for a few minutes by the open door, then approached him.

He felt relieved. Incredibly relieved. He was pedaling easily, going nowhere and not wanting to go anywhere because she was right in front of him. Her hair was in a ponytail. A new pimple was forming on the right side of her chin. She had on a blue skirt, a light blue blouse, white socks and yard sandals.

"You don't want me to check the rest of the answers?" she asked.

"I don't want you to waste your time," he said. The rear wheel whirred.

"Stop pedaling."

He stopped.

"I wanted you to study for this test because I wanted you to learn to think rationally, to look for logical solutions to problems instead of reacting like a caveman."

"I was compensating him," Sonny said. "I was making things equal, giving him my hair for Teresa's."

"You didn't burn Teresa's hair on purpose. It was an accident. And you didn't even do anything to Mr. Ribisi. It wasn't his hair and Teresa didn't want yours. The logical response would have been an apology and a refusal to shave your head."

"Okay."

She glanced at the top of his head.

"It'll grow back," he said.

"You'll never shave it off again?"

"No. And both my grandfathers had full, healthy hair, so I probably won't bald early."

"I'll give you a good shampoo."

"Thanks," he said.

"And you'll never make any other major changes to your body without asking me first?" she asked.

"Like what?"

"Earrings," she said. "Tattoos."

He nodded.

"You don't have to do this anymore," she said.

"I thought you liked watching me ride."

"I wanted you to ride just for me."

"I did," he said.

"You rode to make my father happy, too. I'm tired of sharing your efforts with someone else."

She once calculated the wattage he produced by taping a piece of paper to a rear spoke and counting the number of times it hit the chainstay per minute. "At your peak," she'd said, "you generate enough energy to power a two-hundred-fifty-watt bulb."

He'd always thought of the riding as a necessary means of production. There wouldn't have been the warmth of her tongue without his sweat. No sweat without the bike. No sweetness without the pain.

In the past year he'd powered enough bulbs to light up all of Orange County in the dead of night. Thousands of watts of pure white light that shone for her.

He got off the bike and she kissed him on the lips. "Come on," she said.

"Where are we going?" he asked.

"To shower."

"Us?"

"Yes."

"Together?"

"You studied hard for me. I'm rewarding you." She turned toward the house and a charge sparked in the pit of his stomach and radiated outward until his fingertips and toes tingled, as he imagined what her body looked like, what he would see for the first time in just a minute. Her lower back. The insides of her thighs.

Thank god, he thought as he ran to catch up. Thank sweet Jesus!

He never believed in religion, but years later, shortly after they married, a friend invited Mirla to church and she came home talking about God, Heaven, and other things that no one alive had ever seen, heard, or felt. "How can I believe in something I can't see?" he asked.

She spoke of a life after the physical one, a life of spirits and everlasting joy. She began attending regularly and was angry he wouldn't join her Sunday mornings. She learned to classify their youthful fornication as condemnable. "I'm not saying we're bad people," she said, "but our actions were sinful. Me French-kissing the side of your face. All that premarital sex."

Hell yes, all that premarital sex, he thought.

"We shouldn't have done it," she said.

"Do you even remember what we did?" he asked.

"Unfortunately."

It was the unfortunately that always bothered him. He never understood how she could have felt guilty about something that had felt so good. He never understood how she could have remembered such a wonderful part of their past as sinful, how she could have placed so much faith in beings and places that never existed.

One night on the living room couch, six months pregnant and her belly swollen, Mirla introduced Pascal's wager and recounted how the philosopher-mathematician had believed faith in a Roman Catholic/Judeo-Christian/Western God was a win-win situation.

She pulled out a sheet of notebook paper, set it on the coffee table, and wrote two formulas (where p was the probability of God existing and x was some finite value Sonny didn't exactly understand):

$$\text{Belief in God} \quad = \infty^*p + x_1^*(1 - p) = \infty$$
$$\text{Disbelief in God} = x_2^*p + x_3^*(1 - p) = \text{A finite}$$
$$\text{number}$$
$$\text{nowhere near}$$
$$\text{as good as } \infty$$

"See?" Mirla said. "Belief in God gets you infinite happiness. Disbelief and you go to Hell. So based solely on the probability that He does exist, your best option would be to believe."

"I don't see Hell as the other option. You wrote, 'a finite number.'"

"I know what I wrote. I didn't want to write Hell because I wanted to be encouraging."

"But you just said Hell."

"Because you weren't encouraged."

Sonny looked at the formulas again. He stared at them hard, more for Mirla's sake than his own, before letting out a breath and saying, "You're right."

"So you'll come with me to church?"

"No. But you're right." Then he got up, walked out the front door and down the steps of his apartment building, and stood on the sidewalk. A cool November breeze was blowing. He looked up at the dark sky and the glittering stars and thought, Infinity's just an eight knocked over on its side.

He turned around and saw Mirla above him on the second-floor landing. She stood in front of their open doorway, her beautiful oval form in sihoulette against the yellow living room lights behind her.

I am happy, Sonny thought. Here. Now. This is what I know. Soon I'll have a son or daughter, and I'll never force that child to go to church. Sunday mornings, that child can sleep in with me and we can watch reruns of *The Three Stooges* in the afternoon. I'm a good man and if God exists, and if He is good, then He will not condemn me to Hell. He will know the love I've shown my family, He will forgive me my ignorance, and He will allow me a long, happy life with my child to come and my fanatic wife.

Hard Times on Fairview
(1978–1982)

The apartment Sonny and Mirla shared after their marriage sat near the corner of Fairview and Maywood in a grungy, run-down part of Santa Ana. The building had a flat roof and the stucco exterior was cracked from a combination of a weak, shifting foundation, earthquakes, and age.

The walls of the Fairview apartment complex were covered with graffiti, bubbly red and black letters that said things like WILD BOYZ HERE, JOSÉ RODRIGUEZ SUCKS COCK, and YOU SUCK COCK.

Notable among the graffiti was a crudely painted portrait of Chewbacca that looked like a brown popsicle with black eyes, with bold green letters underneath that proclaimed, VIVA CHUBAKA!

Sonny and Mirla's one-bedroom apartment, with brown shag carpeting that used to be red and which covered the entire six hundred square feet of floor (with the exception of the kitchenette), was known to both the Lum and Ho Families simply as Fairview.

"No, I can't come down to Fairview," and "We heard of a nice vacant apartment somewhere else" became the familial refrains. Even Bo grew concerned and organized a "Fairview Clean-Up" drive at his high school. One Sunday morning, Bo and seven other classmates showed up at Sonny's front door with brushes and canisters of primer and paint. Sonny and Mirla were so surprised by the company that they sat speechless on lawn chairs outside the apartment complex and watched as the teenagers covered the multicolored graffiti sprawl with beige paint.

Though Sonny didn't mind his relations not visiting, it bothered Mirla. In the living room, which doubled as the dining room, she would sit at the Formica table and say over a cup of tea, "If we had guests, I would really enjoy this tea." In bed, she would refuse his advances and sulk, saying, "Why bother? I don't want to get pregnant and raise a child here. She could get sick from the roaches, rats, and ants."

Mirla was a high school math teacher and Sonny worked as a teller at the local Wells Fargo. Though neither of them made a sizable salary, they made enough to move to a better neighborhood. It was Sonny's reluctance to move that upset Mirla even more than the home she wanted to move away from.

"Why are you so attached to this place?" she'd ask every night, and he'd do his best to change the subject.

What Sonny felt he knew was illogical, but felt nonetheless. This was his first apartment, his first home as a single adult out of college, and he loved it.

Yes, the apartment had been burglarized twice with the last incident resulting in blood streaking across the wall and carpet, the burglar having cut himself on the windowsill. Yes, the roar of traffic from the main street outside his bedroom window kept up throughout the night. Yes, their neighbor Vu Tran played loud jazz music upstairs.

But Sonny enjoyed jazz, too, not so much for the music itself as for the atmosphere it generated, the scratchy quality of the records, the trumpets and percussion, these sounds that reminded him of what it was like to be on his own for the first time, listening to Thelonious Monk and Coltrane with Vu after a long day at work.

And no fancy new technology—no cassettes and definitely not one of those boxy Sony tape decks that Bo enjoyed—could replace the sweet, nostalgic feeling produced by a turntable spinning a disc of vinyl.

Sonny was still in his twenties and felt, living in this wild, untamed neighborhood, like a cowboy leading a wagon party out to the prairie West, braving harsh terrain and the assaults of bandits and thieves. Every young man should live through a period of hardship. It built character and besides, word had gotten out around the neighborhood. It'd been months since the last burglary, and since Sonny hid his record player and records in the back of his non-attached garage, there was nothing left in the apartment for a burglar to steal.

"We're safe here," Sonny said to Mirla one night as she pushed his hand off her breast. "The burglars won't come back. They've given up on this place."

"So have I," she said.

Sonny had promised a move immediately after the marriage. Immediately stretched into a month. One month stretched into two, and now, in the third month of their marriage, Sonny faced a choice between a new apartment and celibacy, and that, ultimately, wasn't much of a choice.

Sonny sent a letter to Oregon to notify his landlord of his imminent departure. Mirla had been looking at available apartments since before their marriage, and soon signed a lease on a two-bedroom, second-floor apartment in Garden Grove near her parents' home.

Within weeks they were ready to move in. The atmosphere was festive and both families came by to see the new home the day of the move, bringing with them beer, cake, and chips. "How clean," Mirla's father said. "Wow, no vermin," Sonny's mother, Esther, said.

Mirla stood outside the front door on the landing, surveying the quiet surroundings below.

"There's a neighborhood patrol," she said as Sonny and Larry lugged the sofa up the stairs. "A police car drives by once a week. Isn't that nice?"

He grunted and then said, "Move. Please," as he and Larry carried the sofa in through the front door.

That night she started to make advances toward him, pulling his shirt up over his stomach, but he resisted.

"I don't believe this," she said. "*You're* not in the mood."

"I'm thirsty." He got out of bed and left the room.

He poured himself a glass of water and sat at the kitchen table, sipping from his glass until she came out.

She watched him for a moment. "Most people would be happy not to have a burglar's blood streaking down the walls of their home."

"It wasn't that much blood," he said.

She shook her head in disbelief. "I'm going back to bed."

He followed her back into their room and picked out from the closet *A Love Supreme*. He placed it on the record player at the foot of the bed.

As Coltrane's golden sax lit up "Acknowledgement," Mirla motioned for him to come near.

Normally he would be very happy to see his wife motioning

for him to come near, but this time images of clean sidewalks and perfectly trimmed hedges came to mind, and the music didn't sound as good inside this apartment situated in a neighborhood patrolled regularly by the cops.

She kissed him, then asked, "Why are you frowning?"

"It's nothing," he said.

"What are you thinking about?"

"That some graffiti would really liven up our block."

The bass from Vu's speakers shook the walls. Four years had passed since Sonny's move into the sanitized confines of Garden Grove, and this night in Vu's apartment, Sonny was listening to something that blew his mind.

Grandmaster Flash & the Furious Five's "The Message" was playing on the record player in the living room. Vu and Sonny drank malt liquor on the sofa and looked at the record player, which occupied the central space normally reserved for a TV. Vu often said, "With so much music in the world, who needs a TV?"

Sonny nodded his head to the song.

"This is rap," Vu said. "It'll change the world."

The bass pumped and the beat sounded good to Sonny. Despite the fact they were fairly buzzed, both he and Vu soon began tapping the carpeted floor with their bare feet, in synch.

Every Thursday Sonny spent a couple of hours after work with Vu before returning home. He invited Mirla, but she always chose to stay home with Louis, now three.

"This is great," Sonny said.

"You can borrow it if you want," Vu said.

*   *   *

After putting Louis to bed, Sonny placed the Grandmaster Flash album on the player and then approached Mirla, who looked at the record warily.

As the track played, Sonny began kissing Mirla's neck. Her arms stiffened to his touch, but he persisted, hoping to ease the stress out of her body. He caressed the back of her neck, her shoulders.

After a few moments she said, "Time out," and backed away from him. "What is this?"

"A revolutionary kind of music," Sonny said. "It'll change the world."

She listened to the entire track while Sonny sat across from her on their bed, waiting for the signal to recommence the night of romance.

When the track finished, she said, "Turn that off. Please."

Sonny got up. He took the needle off the record and turned the player off.

She looked concerned.

"When Grandmaster Flash raps about rats and roaches being in the front room, he's making an important comment on the times we live in," Sonny said.

"The times certain disenfranchised people live in," Mirla said. "People living in poverty with few options. We're not in that situation." She paused. "When that Mixmaster—"

"Grandmaster," Sonny said.

"When he talked about the world being a jungle and how he doesn't know if he's going to make it . . . what?"

Sonny's mouth was open.

"What?" Mirla asked again.

"You remembered that line."

"Well, you just played it," she said.

"But you were actually listening."

"Right. What I was saying is that when we're making love, I don't want to think about the world being a jungle and how I'm struggling to survive, because one, I'm not a disenfranchised black man, and two, I don't like to think about social inequality when I'm making love to my husband."

"I can't believe you remembered that line," Sonny said.

Mirla sighed.

"Can I put this on? Just this time?"

Mirla hesitated, then said, "Just this time."

He turned the player back on.

It was a new era in his life, a fortunate time with revolutionary music to accompany it. The needle hit the vinyl, and there was again that comforting scratch and the breathtaking pause before the track began.

The bass pumped, the beat quickened his heart, and he eased toward his wife, pretending her frown was really just intense romantic concentration. As Grandmaster Flash & the Furious Five serenaded the two of them, he caressed her shoulders and slipped off her sky blue nightie, whispering, "Thank you."

What Sonny Did for a Living
(1979-1993)

Louis didn't know.

Calling the Ghosts
(2002)

Louis's father, Sonny, wanted to stop by an Albertson's on the way to Grandma Esther's house. "We can't go empty-handed," he said as Louis pulled into the parking lot.

Inside, his father picked up a case of forty-ounce malt liquor. "For the family," he said, slinging it into the basket. The only people in attendance would be Grandma, Mick, Aunt Helen, his father, and himself. The only person who drank was his father, who also threw in, for the family, a package of doughnuts and beef jerky.

Back in the car, Louis's father popped the cap off a bottle, sniffed the contents, and took a sip. They were still in the parking lot, the key in the ignition, the engine off.

"It's Saturday morning," Louis said. "You want to start drinking now?"

His father motioned for him to start the car.

"You've been watching too many rap videos," Louis said.

"The black ghosts didn't invent malt liquor." His father took another sip. He used the Cantonese phrase "black ghosts" to refer to black people and "white ghosts" to refer to white people. He referred to the Japanese by the Cantonese phrase "turnip heads." The Filipinos were Flips and the Mexicans were Amigos, the only Spanish word he knew. "It's not insulting," he'd explained once. "Amigo means friend. How is that insulting? Don't look at me like that. You think I'm an ignorant old man who doesn't know jack about other cultures."

"What do you have against black people?" Louis asked.

"I have nothing against them," his father said. "I appreciate their contributions to this country."

"Such as?"

"Hip-hop. And Malcolm X."

"Then why don't you just call them black people?" Louis asked.

"Because that's what the Cantonese-speaking people in this world call them. It's standard slang. Most people call a telephone a phone. That's standard. No one argues with that." His father reached over and turned the key, starting the car.

"Just because a lot of people use this slang, and it's outdated slang as well, doesn't mean you need to use it," Louis said.

"You're not as fluent in Cantonese as I am. You don't know the subtleties of the vernacular."

"You've been to Hong Kong twice," Louis said. "You learned your Cantonese from Grandma, the same person I learned it from."

"Get moving."

Louis backed out of the parking space.

"Calling someone a black ghost is not the same as calling him a nigger," his father said. "That's not how I use it."

"Not what I said," Louis said.

"That's what you were getting at. Calling someone a black ghost is like calling him a black guy or a black dude. Slang for the same thing."

"Calling someone a white ghost is like calling him a honky," Louis said.

"Honky means white person. Check the dictionary."

Over the past two months Louis and his father had communicated mostly by banging on counters and tables. They spoke only to contradict each other, and he felt they were better off not talking, because each time his father said black ghost, he remembered the old man's desire to turn Hersey Collins into one.

"When did you start drinking malt liquor?" Louis asked.

His father looked out his window, rubbing the neck of his bottle.

Grandma Esther answered the door in a blue bathrobe. She said hello how are you doing come in. She seemed dazed.

Louis looked at his father, who shrugged.

"Thanks for having us over," Louis said.

"We brought food," his father said, indicating the beef jerky, doughnuts, and malt liquor he held in two plastic grocery bags.

Grandma looked at the liquor.

"The drinks aren't for you, Ah-Mah," his father said.

"This isn't food, Sonny," she said.

"They're for me and Louis, and Mick."

"You drink?" Grandma asked Louis.

"No."

"Has Mick started drinking?" she asked.

"No."

She frowned at his father, who frowned at him.

"Come in," she said.

Mick and Aunt Helen hadn't arrived yet.

"Sit down." They sat at the dining room table and his father set his bags down next to the fried turnip cakes, egg rolls, and sliced watermelons that were already there. Grandma gave the doughnuts and beef jerky a slight nudge to distance them from her food.

The room was still beige. Beige carpet, beige walls, and the inverted pincushion of a glassy chandelier above.

The turnip cakes were steaming and the smell of beef and onions made Louis's mouth water. Grandma's turnip cakes usually settled like bricks in his stomach. They gave his father heartburn and Mick the runs. She used a recipe supposedly passed down through many generations of her family, the Hsiehs. The Lums of Orange County had always approached her turnip cakes with a sense of dread, but Louis was hungry now and hunger was an irresistible spice. He picked up his chopsticks and dug in.

By the time Mick and Aunt Helen arrived, Louis had eaten most of the turnip cakes and egg rolls.

Mick wore a wife-beater shirt and tan khakis. He worked out four days a week, two hours a day, and looked like an action figure come to life. His biceps and triceps were chiseled and robust. Veins crawled up his thick neck.

Louis believed Mick lifted as intensely as he did to prove the death curse theory wrong, to prove he would survive to old age through physical strength and endurance. He stood five-eleven, weighed two hundred fifteen pounds, and walked with such authority Louis sometimes believed the only things capable of killing him were his own veiny hands. Louis liked to think of his cousin as indestructible.

Mick sold real estate and had made enough money from the past five years to buy a 2200-square-foot house in Huntington Beach, which he'd shared with his girlfriend Regan until they broke up. He worked six days a week and kept in touch with old clients. Taped to his cubicle wall were words he'd written for himself: "There is enough time in every day to sell a house. Every day is a potentially good day."

"What's a bad day?" Louis had asked.

"Calling an old client and hearing the word foreclosed."

Mick's home had a pool, a theater system in the living room, and a billiards table. After Regan moved out, Mick bought a doghouse equipped with two rooms and purple carpeting. "What I really need," he said, "is a dog."

When he wasn't working, lifting weights, or hanging out with old college friends, Mick visited pet stores and played with the dogs kenneled there, rubbing their bellies and shaking their paws, looking for his furry soul mate as any other twenty-eight-year-old might be looking for a human companion in a bar, club, or church. "A golden retriever is a fine beast," Mick often said. "They're quiet and obedient. Not like beagles. A beagle will yap your ears off and piss on your feet."

He said, and this made sense to Louis, that the only beings capable of giving unconditional love were parents and dogs. "A dog will come back and lick your face even after you've yelled at it or slapped it on the ass for doing something wrong. He'll whimper and stop wagging his tail for a minute or two, but he'll always come back to you."

"Why don't you just take one home?" Louis asked.

"Not ready for the commitment. I'd have to bring him with me wherever I go, or find a sitter if I leave on a trip."

At the previous Lum family meeting, Grandma had said to Mick, "Your father and Uncle Sonny already had children when they were your age. When am I going to see some great-grand-children?"

"Soon as Louis gets on the ball."

"Granduncle Phil didn't marry until he was forty-five," Louis had said.

"He was a scientist who created an important medicine for mankind. He didn't have time to get married." According to Grandma, Granduncle Phil had created diphenhydramine hydrochloride back in the forties and sold it to Parke-Davis, who marketed the formula as Benadryl.

"I'm a scientist of real estate," Mick had said.

"You're not creating Benadryl," Grandma had said. It was a saying Mick enjoyed hearing very much. He used it frequently himself. If, for example, Louis was too busy to have lunch with him, Mick would say, "You're not creating Benadryl." Too tired to play tennis at the park? You're not creating Benadryl. Complaining about a long day at work? You're not creating Benadryl.

Now that everyone had arrived, Grandma sat down at the head of the table. Mick and Aunt Helen sat across from Louis and his father, and surveyed the food.

Aunt Helen wore her hair short and combed to one side. She had on a plain gray sweater. Mick nodded at Louis. "What's up?" He looked at Louis's father. "Hey Uncle Sonny."

Louis's father saluted him with his bottle of malt liquor. It was the same bottle he'd been working on in the car.

"When did you start drinking forties?" Mick asked.

"Eat," Grandma said. There were five egg rolls and half a turnip cake left. The sliced watermelons were plentiful. The packages of beef jerky and powdered doughnuts were unopened.

"No, thanks," Mick said. "I'm not hungry." Aunt Helen winced at the spread, like the food was going to eat her.

"You've been told he's alive," Mick said. "What's the problem?"

"I need to hear him tell me," Grandma said.

Nobody responded.

"None of you is worried something could have happened to him?" she asked.

"He used to lock his bedroom door and stay inside for hours," Louis's father said. "On weekends."

"He didn't have many friends when he was young. He didn't have a reason to be outside."

"Every kid has a reason to be outside," Louis's father said.

"Not every kid was as disobedient as you," Grandma said.

"You usually ask us if we've been ill," Aunt Helen said. "You usually ask us if we're happy. How about asking us how we're doing?"

"Stop giving her a hard time," Mick said to his mother.

Grandma glared at Aunt Helen. "So none of you cares whether he's dead or alive?"

"He's alive," Louis's father said. "He wants to be left alone. He's always wanted to be left alone. Since he first developed consciousness and realized he was happier alone than with people."

"If you were nicer to him, he would have been more comfortable around people," Grandma said.

Louis's father looked angry, like he was going to shout. Aunt Helen and Mick looked excited by the prospect of an argument.

The old man bit his lip.

"Not one of you gives a shit," Grandma said.

Louis was shocked, not by Grandma cursing, though that was new. A tear had appeared and trailed down her face. These were two firsts in two days—her trembling voice on the answering machine the previous night and now her tears. "Grandma's crying." He hadn't meant to say it out loud.

"No shit," Mick said. "Go grab her a paper towel from the kitchen."

Grandma wiped her face quickly with the back of her hand. "Sit down, Louis."

Her crying made him uncomfortable. He'd always been uncomfortable seeing family members in vulnerable states, like the time his father fell off his mountain bike, tumbled down a hill, and snapped his collarbone. He was nine and haunted by the sight of his old man in a sling, shifting uncomfortably in bed, calling out for his wife to bring him more soup and bread, moaning.

"It'll heal," his mother had said. "It doesn't even hurt. Your father has no tolerance for pain." Louis avoided his father until the sling came off, going out to the yard if the old man was watching TV, coming in to watch TV if he went out to the yard.

Grandma had been steady through all the deaths in her family. Her crying now was unnatural. "I'm flying to Hong Kong to look for him," she said.

"Hong Kong's a big mess of a city," Mick said. "You're going to get mugged."

"That's why I could use some company," she said.

"This is the busiest time of the year for me," Aunt Helen said. "I can't leave work now."

Mick said he couldn't just up and go. "I have clients who need me to be here. But I will fund your trip. I'll cover any expenses for you and whoever chooses to go with you, because an old woman shouldn't be walking around Hong Kong by herself." He nodded at Louis to volunteer. "You don't even like your job."

"Yes I do," Louis said.

"Do you have any vacation time, Uncle Sonny?"

"No," Louis's father said. "Give him a few months, Ah-Mah. If you don't hear from him, then let's talk again."

Louis thanked Grandma for the food.

"Nobody's worried about him," she said. "Unbelievable. Everybody's more worried about work."

Louis looked down at the table. He could feel everyone else looking down, too. He glanced at his father. The old man's face was turning a deep red. The bottle he'd been working on since the drive over was only half empty.

The old man burped.

Aunt Helen sneezed.

"Bless you."

"Thanks, Louis."

"Do you need a tissue, Mom?" Mick asked.

"Sit down, Mick," Grandma said. "I'm glad you liked the food, Louis. Take the rest with you."

The sight of Grandma crying stuck in Louis's mind as he drove home. His old man was snoring, his head pressed against the window. He'd drunk only half of the forty and poured the rest down Grandma's sink. He'd knocked himself out on a twenty and now clung to the rest of the case in his lap.

Louis wondered why his father wouldn't volunteer to take a couple of weeks off and fly to Hong Kong, if just to make Grandma happy. He was a bank manager, but Louis hadn't known that when he wrote his seventh-grade family history report. The night before it was due, he'd asked his father what he did.

"I work."

"What kind of work?"

"Hard work." The old man was getting ready for bed and Louis didn't want to keep him up with questions.

He worried that Mrs. Keller might give him a lower grade for writing "hard work," so he assigned his father a profession. He wrote, "Born in 1950, Sonny Lum worked for the IRS," to which Mrs. Keller wrote in her response, "Your father's in a great position of power!"

Louis hadn't meant to put his father in a position of power. He'd chosen the IRS because the week before, he'd overheard his father saying, "The fucking IRS is stealing from me."

His father had occupied one line in his report, but one line was enough to convince Mrs. Keller that his father could be used in the same sentence with the words great and power.

Louis had never thought of his old man in those terms. He'd never thought much of his father outside the context of his own life. He'd never wondered what his father did when they weren't together in the house, eating and watching TV. He'd never wondered what radio station his father listened to on his way to work, what he ate for lunch, or what he thought of his coworkers. These details helped define a man and Louis didn't know a single one, and hadn't cared to know.

What he knew was that a man was the sum of his actions. His father was now sleeping off a twenty of malt liquor. He reeked of alcohol. When sober, he called people ghosts and threatened to kill Hersey Collins.

Louis felt like the dog of Mick's dreams, an obedient beast who chauffeured his drunk father and watched him to make sure he stayed away from knives and other potentially lethal objects. He couldn't stand to live with this man anymore. In the wild, old male lions chased the young ones out of their prides. This was the natural way. The old and young should not be cohabiting the same space.

His father was still snoring when they pulled up the driveway.

Louis walked around to the passenger side, looked at the old man's face mashed against the window, and considered leaving him in the car.

He opened the door slowly and pulled the case of forties off him. He set it on the driveway and shook him awake.

"What?"

"We're home," Louis said, helping him out.

His father leaned against him. "You need to lose twenty pounds," Louis said. His father grunted in response.

They went inside and Louis led him to his room and into bed. He shut the door behind him and went back out to the driveway, where he emptied the rest of the malt liquor on the front lawn. Then he drove to Grandma's house.

A Great Time to Be Alive
(1990-2002)

In the summer of the year 1281, Lum Sung Sung was conscripted off a Chinese fishing junk and sent with the invading Mongol fleet to Japan. After landing in Hakata Bay, he deserted his army in the night and hid in the nearby woods. The Mongols engaged the defending samurais in a series of skirmishes before a typhoon wiped out the anchored invading fleet, plunging men and horses into the bottom of the sea. Without a ride home, Sung Sung, or $Sung^2$ as Uncle Bo called him in his report, wandered Japan looking for a ship to take him back to China.

Everything Louis knew about $Sung^2$ he discovered from Uncle Bo. And everything he knew was only half the story because Uncle Bo had composed just fifty-five handwritten pages before he stopped writing. He never found out how $Sung^2$ had successfully returned home.

In the fifth grade, Louis wrote his uncle as part of a pen pal assignment. "Pick someone who lives far from you," his teacher had said.

Louis figured that the farther the person lived, the better grade he'd receive, so he picked as far as possible.

Uncle Bo wrote, "Dear Nephew, I'm flattered you're asking me to be part of your project. It's a great time to be alive!" He wished Louis and his family well, said he was healthy and happy in Hong Kong, said he'd met a beautiful woman named Julie with whom he watched Disney cartoons, and included a brief account of Sung^2's life, which began by proclaiming him a brave hero in their family line.

Uncle Bo described Sung^2 as "one who ran from a battle the way a starving man runs toward food."

Louis could relate. He supported pacifism, which he understood as running away from all potential harm whenever possible. Harm in the fifth grade took the form of Gary Gonzalez, who possessed the thick, hairy body of a well-built, thirty-year-old man, and who enjoyed tying Louis and his friends to the chin-up bars with rope. Harm also took the shape of Miranda Gonzalez, Gary's sister, who also possessed the body of a well-built, thirty-year-old man, and who enjoyed pulling Louis into the girl's bathroom so she could smother him with kisses and call him her Little Muchacho, the black hairs on her forearms chafing his cheeks as she pulled him close.

Uncle Bo began sending Louis addenda to the original account of Sung^2, followups and corrections he'd gathered from research at various libraries and museums in Hong Kong. He asked Louis for feedback, whether he found the story moving, interesting, or boring. Louis admired his ancestor for running and hiding from conflict, and believed he'd been descended from this man. He wrote Uncle Bo about school:

"I finally beat Jason Hahn. He missed methamphetamine. Such an easy word. I represented my school in the county spelling bee and finished third. I believe spelling is my calling."

Uncle Bo sent responses:

"Good on finishing third. Looks like your plan to memorize nine thousand new words over summer vacation paid off. I drank a toast to your success. Julie sends her congratulations. Here are a few more pages on Sung^2."

Uncle Bo provided answers, counseling, and advice on everything Louis presented before him:

"She punches you because she's attracted to you. When you say she looks like a man, does that include broad shoulders? Does she have a deep voice?

"A C in geography is meaningless. Unless you become a cartographer, you don't need to know where the United Arab Emirates is. Julie says don't worry about it, and she works in a museum.

"Don't hide the dirty pictures under your mattress. Keep them folded inside one of your encyclopedias. The H–I or I–L edition; anywhere in the middle of the alphabet is a safe spot.

"Just because she likes Tuan now doesn't mean you did anything wrong. This was a girl who used to force you to make out with her in the bathroom, and a girl with broad, mannish shoulders as well. Best you let that sort go."

They talked on the phone a handful of times, and the only images Louis had of his uncle were from old pictures in which he was a thin man with a head full of wavy black hair. From their conversations and from his letters, Uncle Bo came across as a perpetually cheery person. He offered agreeable advice and support from a distant land. He never gave the stares of rebuke, exasperated sighs, or winces Louis's parents would make when he brought home C's in geography.

And what Uncle Bo gave in support Louis returned. Whenever Uncle Bo wrote, "Are you sure you like this section about Sung^2?" he responded with an enthusiastic yes and a request for more, even though intricate descriptions of straw tatamis, wooden shojis, and leather samurai armor were slow and uninteresting. What he found most interesting were Uncle Bo's descriptions of his own life in Hong Kong.

Uncle Bo first met Julie at the Hong Kong Museum of Art. She was a docent leading his tour group through the Antiquities Section.

"I noticed she was a beauty when she pointed out a white marble Guanyin from the Eastern Wei dynasty," Uncle Bo wrote. "She smiled at me when we passed by the palm-sized red lacquer boxes from the Yuan dynasty. I asked her out next to a Ming dynasty jade water jar shaped like a dragon-headed tortoise. She told me to wait while she answered questions from the other tour members who were asking about scrolls and dresses. When we reached the Qing dynasty, she stood in front of an ivory snuff bottle and told me she would be busy that night. She led us on and pointed at a libation cup made out of a rhinoceros horn. It was painted red with dragons carved around the outside in relief, and there at the end of the Qing dynasty, I realized I would marry her."

Uncle Bo soon became a regular of her museum tours and convinced her to agree to a date. More dates followed. They eventually married and honeymooned in Thailand, where they rode elephants. Louis was happy for his uncle's happiness. He delighted at each description Uncle Bo provided of Julie— her ability to perfectly mimic the monkey from *Aladdin,* for example.

After she died, Uncle Bo stopped writing and the story of Sung[2]'s journey, at fifty-five pages, was left unfinished.

He wrote his uncle.

"How did Sung[2] get home? When he was away, did his family believe he was dead? Did they hold a funeral service for him? Did a lot of people attend?

114

"Are you still doing research at the library?

"Exercise. It's good to sweat when you're upset."

His father asked him to stop writing. "Yes, I mean no more letters until he writes you. He wants to be left alone. Nobody's at fault. I don't know when he'll write back."

Every afternoon Louis checked the mailbox, hoping for a letter from Uncle Bo. He asked Grandma Esther if she had any contact with him.

"I have his address, but he told me not to visit," she said. "I have his number, but he told me not to call. I send him a form. He fills it out. He's alive. He has a job and continues to plan on waking the next day. That's good enough for me."

A year passed. Uncle Bo could fill out Grandma's forms, but not write him a letter. He tried to forget his uncle as his uncle had probably forgotten about him. But he couldn't forget and so he put to good use what had been written.

He plagiarized sections of Sung[2]'s life for his seventh-grade family history report, the majority of which covered the Mongolian invasion of Japan. Mrs. Keller wrote, "I appreciate your ambition in reaching so far back into history, but don't you think fourteen pages (out of twenty) on the Mongols is a bit much? What about your family today? (I really did enjoy your technical discussion of ancient flamethrowers and catapults, though.)" She gave him an A minus, the A for vivid details of Mongolian cavalry and weapons, the minus for writing so little on his family in the twentieth century.

He plagiarized the report again in high school for a research paper on genealogy. By college, Louis had dismissed Sung[2]'s life as fiction. He dismissed it as easily as Uncle Bo had dismissed him. He dismissed it to spite his uncle, who had had years to grieve, enough time to write a note or a letter. "Hi Louis, sorry I didn't write back," he could've written, or "Hi Louis, how have you been?"

Was he dead or alive? Was he still in Hong Kong?

Louis had always taken comfort in knowing the facts. He enjoyed verifying names, dates, and numbers. It was what made his editorial assistant work fun despite the meager paycheck. His father was Sonny and his mother Mirla. Grandpa had blown Nazis away with a machine gun in France. Death looked like Grandpa and had wiped out half the Orange County Lums. The word cleave suggested coming together or apart. Louis knew all this and once knew he'd been descended from Lum Sung Sung.

He'd given Uncle Bo the benefit of the doubt. He'd believed his uncle would finish the story of Sung^2's life, which he'd presented as the main focus of his family history report. It was Sung^2 who'd been featured, not Granduncle Phil and his discovery of diphenhydramine hydrochloride, not his mother and her high school math exploits, and definitely not Grandpa and his stint in France. He'd believed his uncle had cared enough to share a piece of family history the other Lums didn't know about. He'd believed his uncle would at least write back to let him know he wouldn't be writing anymore, and the man never did.

Point of Departure
(2002)

Esther was surprised to see him. "Come in. How are you doing?"

"Fine," Louis said. He followed her into the living room and sat down on the sofa. She sat next to him.

"Your father shouldn't drink so much."

"He didn't drink much at all."

"You look confused," she said.

"You always say 'your father,' when you talk about my father, but you don't say 'your uncle,' when you talk about Uncle Bo. You say Bo."

"Sonny's your father. If Bo had a son, I'd say 'your father' to that boy, too."

Louis thought it over. "I want to go to Hong Kong and look for Uncle Bo. I want to go alone."

"I'm not an invalid," she said. "I won't slow you down."

"You have to stay here and watch your son."

"You said he's okay," Esther said.

"I didn't say that. You assumed it."

"What's wrong with him?" she asked.

"He wants to kill the man who killed Mom."

"How long has he felt like this?"

"A long time."

"He's depressed," she said.

"He's thinking about murdering someone. That's not just being depressed."

"Fine."

"He's your son," Louis said. There was anger in his voice.

"I know that."

"You've known him longer than I have," Louis said. "You raised him. You told him what he could and couldn't do for eighteen years. If I had your experience, I'd try to figure out a way to change his mind. He won't listen to me. There's a chance he'll listen to you. He's crazy."

"Don't call him crazy," she said.

"He's a freaking lunatic."

"You're right. You haven't known him as long as I have. Don't call him a freaking lunatic."

"Then what is he?"

"Don't call him those names," she said.

"My Cantonese is passable. I'm good with directions. I walk fast. I'll find out what happened to Uncle Bo, but you have to stay with Dad."

"You think he'd do it?" she asked.

"I moved in with him because he said he would."

"Maybe he just wants company. Maybe he doesn't really want to do it."

"Maybe he does," Louis said.

"You've done a generous thing by watching over him," she said.

"If I have to watch over him much longer, I'll kill Hersey Collins myself."

"Why do you want to find your uncle?" she asked. This was important. If she was going to stay and watch Sonny, and hand the search to Louis, she needed to know he would see it through to its conclusion.

"He never responded to the last letter I sent him," Louis said. "He owes me an explanation."

"I understand."

Louis's father was pouring a glass of milk. It was four in the morning. "What are you doing up?"

"Getting something to drink," Louis said.

"Here."

"Thanks."

"Welcome."

"I'm leaving," Louis said.

His father checked the clock on the microwave. "Going out for a breakfast burrito? Grab me one."

"I'm going to look for Uncle Bo in Hong Kong. I talked to Grandma about it last night. She agreed to let me go by myself."

"He's alive," his father said. "You don't need to look for him."

"I want to."

"I'm making you so miserable you're leaving the country?" his father asked.

"It's not only because of you."

"When I said your mother was like my right leg, I meant she was very, very important to me. I could have said she was like my heart, but I wouldn't have meant that. The legs are two of the most important parts of the body."

"Okay."

"You think I've insulted her," his father said.

"It's too early in the morning to argue."

"What I said about her was the highest compliment I could give anyone. That's what I'm saying."

"Fine," Louis said. "I believe you."

"You don't." His father walked to his room.

"I'm going out for a breakfast burrito," Louis said. "You want one?"

"No."

Louis left and when he returned, music was pumping from his father's room, the bass quaking the walls. He knocked on his father's door. The music stopped and the door opened. "What?"

"Breakfast burrito," Louis said.

"I said I didn't want one."

"Here."

His father took it. "Thanks."

"What were you listening to?" Louis asked.

His father motioned for him to come in.

On the bed was an album by someone named Biz Markie. In front of the closet was a stack of vinyl records. "You can take a look if you want."

Louis knelt down and flipped through them. The album covers all featured black men. Some wore red Adidas jumpsuits and gold chains around their necks. Some didn't. Some looked pissed off. Some didn't. They were Grandmaster Flash & Furious Five, Rhythm Heritage, Afrika Bambaataa, Eric B. & Rakim, Run DMC, Public Enemy, and more. Some he'd heard of, most he hadn't. "When did you start drinking malt liquor?"

"Years ago," his father said.

"Who introduced you to it?" Louis asked.

"A neighbor."

"Where were you living?"

"Santa Ana."

"I'd like to have one pleasant conversation with you before I leave," Louis said.

"I was living a mile down from where you were living, on Fairview."

"Nice place?"

"A shithole like your place was," his father said. "It was burglarized twice before I moved out.

"The first time it happens, I come home and the place is a mess. My neighbor Vu comes downstairs and knocks on my door. Says he's sorry. Says he saw them take my stuff. Says he should have called the cops, but was afraid the burglars would come back and kill him.

"I tell him I would have called the cops if I was in his place. You can't live your life in fear, I say. They took my goddamn mattress.

"Says he feels terrible about not making the call. I sleep on the floor with the roaches, I tell him. I don't even have a bowl for rice. He leaves and comes back with a couple bottles of malt liquor. Says it's all the food he has."

"I never knew you lived so close to my old place," Louis said.

"Your mother didn't allow alcohol in the house. She didn't like hip-hop, either. She thought the bass would make her go deaf. She wanted a quiet house with no alcohol, and I respected her preferences. She was so happy when you started listening to REO Speedwagon."

"Were you always this bad a drinker?" Louis asked.

"Takes time to build up tolerance, boy."

"Your tolerance was much higher before?"

"Yeah."

"When you used to drink regularly?" Louis asked.

"Yeah."

"Really?" Louis asked.

"I said yeah."

"You plan to keep drinking it?" Louis asked.

"You poured what I had on the front lawn."

"You plan on buying more?"

"Malt liquor tastes like crap," his father said.

"Why'd you buy a case?" Louis asked.

"I liked the idea I could keep it in the house. I didn't think you'd react like your mother."

"Sorry."

"I'm thinking of switching to gin anyway," his father said. "It's healthier."

Louis put the records down. If his father had told him the malt liquor story years before, he could have included it in his family history report, and his father would have occupied more than one line.

His father plucked a record from the stack and put it on the turntable. "I'll play you a standard."

"It's called 'A Standard'?" Louis asked.

It was called "Rapper's Delight." As the track played, his father nodded his head to the beat and his lips approximated a smile. After it finished, his father asked, "You coming back in a few weeks?"

"Your burrito's getting cold," Louis said.

His father paused, like he wanted to repeat his question, then unwrapped his breakfast and took a bite. "This is different from my usual."

"It's a deluxe," Louis said.

"What's in a deluxe?"

"Eggs and sausage. Bell peppers. Onions. Beans."

"I don't like bell peppers," his father said.

Esther called Hong Kong again. "Tell me where he is," she said to the landlady.

"I can't. He made me promise not to."

"You're killing me."

"Please," the landlady said.

"I've had two open-heart surgeries. My husband died in World War II and I raised Bo all by myself. But I don't want pity. I just want to hear his voice one last time before I die."

"Can't you take comfort in knowing he's alive?" the landlady asked. "You can ask a hundred times and I'll tell you a hundred times he's alive and in good health."

"That's not good enough," Esther said.

"Please see a doctor if you have pain."

"You cold, cold dog."

"He's safe."

"You don't deserve to be a mother," Esther said.

"He loves you."

"Heartless rat."

The landlady refused to reveal what she knew over the phone, and would refuse again in followup conversations that adhered to the same pattern—request for information, refusal to provide information, insult landlady, request for information again, refusal again, insult landlady again.

Esther believed that when the landlady saw that a member of Bo's family had flown thousands of miles to search for him, she'd no doubt feel so guilty she'd have to reveal where Bo was.

"That's what you're counting on?" Louis asked. "You're counting on her to have a change of heart just because I'm knocking on her door?"

"She's a mother. She understands my concern. And you'll knock on her door every night until she tells you. You can go sightseeing during the day, but at night you knock on her door."

"What if she calls the cops?" Louis asked.

"She won't do that. She's never hung up on me even after I called her names."

"You called her names?"

Esther wanted physical proof that Bo was alive and well.

"A photo's good, right?" Louis asked.

"Best if I can talk to him. Next best thing would be a picture you take of him. Bring me a shirt. A pair of pants. Physical evidence. You have enough pocket money?"

"I've got enough for three weeks," Louis said.

"What if it takes more than three weeks?"

"If the landlady won't tell me in three weeks, she won't tell me."

"She'll tell you," Esther said.

"I hope so. My boss only gave me three weeks off."

"We're here," Sonny said. Louis was next to him, Ah-Mah in the backseat.

"Don't park in the lot," Louis said. "Just pull up to the curb."

"I'm not going to leave you at the curb."

"You can't walk me in anyway. See the guards with the automatic rifles? You can't walk past check-in anymore unless you have a boarding pass. Security's changed."

There was gridlock. Cars were stuck end to end, side by side, slowly circling the LAX terminals.

"Then I'll walk you as far as I can," Sonny said.

"That would be the curb," Louis said.

Sonny groaned. He pulled over and a guard checked the trunk. They stepped out and Louis removed his black tote bag and brown suitcase from the car. He set them on the ground and hugged his grandmother.

"Have a safe flight," Sonny said, and patted him on the arm.

"I'll call you when I land," Louis said.

"Have a safe flight," Sonny said again.

"I will."

"Louis," Sonny said.

"Jesus. I'll have a safe flight." Louis slung his bag over his shoulder and lifted his suitcase.

"Request a seat next to an emergency exit," Sonny said.

"I was going to do that anyway."

"And make sure you know how to use the oxygen mask," Sonny said.

"I do."

"It's a long flight," Ah-Mah said.

"Don't worry about it. I want to find him and make you happy."

"Is that true?" Ah-Mah asked.

"And I need to get out of the country for a while."

"Can you say that again?" Ah-Mah asked.

"I need to get out of the country for a while."

"What you said before," Ah-Mah said.

"I want to make you happy?" Louis asked.

"Say it again."

"I want to make you happy."

She smiled.

"Are you okay, Ah-Mah?" Sonny asked.

"Quiet," she said. "One more time."

"I want to make you happy," Louis said.

"Thank you."

"You still remember your Cantonese, right?" Sonny asked.

"Yeah, it's great," Louis said. A pause. "It's passable." Another pause. "I'm sure people there speak English."

His son gave them a final wave. Then he turned and walked past the armed guards, through the sliding glass doors, and out of sight.

Speaking Cantonese So-So Okay
(1990)

Louis believed he spoke Cantonese much better than so-so okay, which was how Grandma, who taught him the dialect, described his proficiency in it.

There were seven tones, three more than in Mandarin. Speaking correctly was not only a matter of pronouncing the correct word. It involved pronouncing the correct word with the correct intonation. High. High rising. High falling. Middle. Low. Low rising. Low falling.

Every Saturday between the ages of eight and fourteen, Louis learned Cantonese from Grandma, which was to say every Saturday she popped into her cassette player one of a series of Cantonese instructional tapes, pressed play, and went to the patio to read while he listened.

The series was entitled *How Are You, Willy Lau?* and featured the travels of Willy Lau and his son Joseph. They launched off Cape Canaveral in a space shuttle with the mission of foresting the moon. They buckled on steel armor, polished their scabbards, and sailed westward for the Americas on Spanish galleons. They joined Roman legions in repelling hordes of fur-covered Vandals in the woods of what is now Germany. They went to the San Diego Zoo (*"Ah-Bah, paau!* Father, leopard!").

Louis considered himself a capable speaker of Cantonese, and dismissed Grandma's winces at his tones because he believed he spoke the Queen's English of Cantonese and she spoke Cockney.

His mother often took him to Chinatown for Saturday grocery trips when he was in grade school. They'd walk past fruit markets and herbal shops and she'd point at random people and say, "They're speaking Cantonese. Listen. You'll never learn if all you listen to are tapes."

On the corner of Alpine and Broadway was the tea seller's shop, and there the shop owner's conversations with the retired old locals often became heated. Louis's mother would stop by the small, two-story building to listen. Stacked on the main counter near the entrance were rows of large clear jars that contained everything from tea leaves to dried seahorses and abalone. The scent of ginseng and mushrooms filled the room.

"Two hundred dollars a pound?" one of the old locals would ask.

"Monkey-picked leaves, ignoramus."

"Monkey leaves?"

"Nobody asked you to like the price."

"These leaves aren't worth two hundred pounds of monkey turd."

"Your mother's a monkey."

"Suck on my asshole."

"Fuck you and your monkey mother!"

Cantonese was a tricky language. It was a hard dialect with sharp, bitting sounds. Mandarin was gentle in comparison, too soft. Cantonese was a commanding dialect, fit for someone who gave orders.

At age eight, Louis wrapped a white T-shirt around the top of his head and fashioned himself captain of a galleon. He gave orders to the stuffed animals in his room. To the pig he commanded, "Swing the tiller six degrees west and watch that mainsail!" He used words he remembered from Chinatown and the tapes. "Bring me a goblet of your finest wine, ignoramus!" he shouted at the dalmatian, its eyes frozen wide in surprised joy. To his disbelieving parents he said, "Don't stand there like blocks of wood. Mop the deck!"

Different tones produced different meanings. *Saangchoi* with a high tone on -*choi* meant lettuce. *Saangchoi* with a low tone on -*choi* meant make money. Louis's mother had plenty of the former and was never satisfied with her proficiency at the latter.

Different modifiers produced different meanings using the same base word. *Fong-bihn* meant convenient. *Daaih-bihn* meant take a shit.

One had to be careful not to substitute lettuce for money, convenience for shit.

When he was eleven, Louis asked to go to the San Diego Zoo. His father decided to take him to the one in Santa Ana. It was smaller and much closer to home. "San Diego's ticket prices are way too high," his father said. "A bird in San Diego is the same as a bird in Santa Ana."

The Santa Ana Zoo housed mostly barnyard animals. There were several lambs encrusted in dried mud, a bony cow, and a red-eyed, quivering white bunny that looked like it had the DTs.

They stopped at one exhibit, his mother on his right side, his father on his left. Louis pointed at the creature behind the steel fence. It was sunning itself on a rock and gnawing on a sprig of weed. "*Ah-Bah, paau!*"

"Tone's decent," his mother said.

His father sighed, then said in English, "That's not a leopard. That's a goat."

Gin and Juice
(2002)

Of all her sons, Sonny was the one who looked most like Melvin. They all resembled Melvin when they were babies, with their wide square faces and thin lips. But Sonny, as a baby, *was* Melvin. The resemblance was so close Melvin began calling him Sonny before they decided on a name. "My Sonny. Look at my Sonny." He held their boy, whose head was covered with splotches of red and blue, bruised by the metal forceps used to pry him from her body.

Esther, panting, thought from where she lay, My Sonny my ass. You're just the damn cheerleader. I did all the hard work.

"My Sonny," Melvin said. "My Sonny."

In response, Sonny pissed on his father and let out a wail. Esther smiled. My Sonny, she thought.

Now fifty-two, Sonny was unhappy with the idea of her moving into his house. "You're not staying long," he said as he carried her bags into Louis's room. He put them down next to the bed.

"Do you really want to kill the man?" she asked.

"Yes."

"You can say you don't want to kill him, and you could have said it to Louis if you really didn't want us here."

"It wouldn't be true."

"Is it just because you need company? I don't mind staying if that's the only reason. I'd feel better knowing you aren't really thinking about killing him."

"I think about it," he said.

"You're stronger than me," she said. "If you decide to do it, how will I stop you?"

"I don't know."

"Does my staying here help make you feel like you shouldn't do it?"

He shrugged.

"It's been less than a year," she said. "You'll get used to being alone." She meant to sound encouraging, not resigned to unhappiness, but Sonny winced and she immediately regretted her words.

For a few days they didn't talk except to announce dinner or say hello or good-bye in passing. The fourth night she sat by him on the sofa as he watched TV.

"Stop staring at me," he said.

"I haven't seen your face up close in a long time. You have good skin. Hardly any blemishes."

"You're making me nervous." He took a sip of his bottle. His refrigerator held a case of Seagram's Lemon Splash, a carton of milk, and a bottle of ranch dressing.

"There's no food here," she said.

"We have cereal."

"Just that and alcohol."

"And milk," he said. "What?"

"Give me sip of that."

"It's not good for someone your age," he said.

"Alcohol thins the blood. I take pills to do the same thing."

"Are you sure?" he asked.

"Yes."

He handed her his bottle and she took a sip. It tasted like lemonade mixed with alcohol, and wasn't nearly as strong as the 120-proof Chinese rice wine Melvin used to bring home. He'd bought the liquor from a Chinatown merchant who'd refused to sell anything below a hundred proof.

"How's it?" Sonny asked.

"Fruity."

"It's fruit-flavored," he said.

"That's what I meant," she said.

He went to the kitchen and returned with a new bottle for her. "Here."

"I didn't mean fruity like it's a weak drink," she said, giving his back.

"Are you worried I'll get caught and sentenced to death," Sonny asked, "or that you'll be seen as the mother of a murderer?"

"I don't think you'll be happier if you kill him."

He was still working on his first bottle when she finished hers. His face was red and the alcohol seeped from his skin and permeated the air.

"You want another one?" he asked.

"No, thanks." She liked the fruity taste. She could have gone for another, but decided not to. It'd embarrass him to watch her out-drink him.

"You think about me being happy?" he asked.

"Yes," she said.

"You think about Louis being happy?"

"Yes."

"And Mick?" he asked.

She nodded.

"Even Helen?"

She nodded again.

"Honestly?" he asked.

"No."

"Do you often think about Ah-Bah?" he asked.

"Yes."

"Because you never seemed happy with him," he said. "You were usually upset at me and Larry. You only seemed happy around Bo, and I used to think it was because out of us three he looked the least like Ah-Bah."

"I was happy with how all my sons looked."

"But were you happy with the way Ah-Bah looked?"

"He looked satisfactory," she said.

"Satisfactory. That's how you'd describe a bowel movement."

"I didn't want a very handsome man. A very handsome man will cheat on a woman."

"You're calling him ugly," Sonny said.

"I said he wasn't very handsome. That doesn't mean ugly. He had broad shoulders and they were beautiful enough."

Sonny smirked.

"What?" she asked.

"I can't believe you were attracted to him," Sonny said. "I can't imagine you two had any romance. I used to think you two had to drink a lot before you had sex. That strong stuff."

She slapped him on the back of his head.

He laughed.

They didn't speak for a few minutes. They watched TV. Australian rules football was on and men with no shoulder pads and no helmets smashed into each other with their thick, powerful bodies.

"Sonny?" She tapped him on the shoulder.

He'd fallen asleep. She wanted to tell him she thought about Melvin all the time. She thought about how comfortable his shoulders had been to rest against in bed. She thought about how he'd slap her on the bottom as he passed by on the way to get a beer from the fridge, a soft tap as if to say, Hey pal.

She took the bottle out of Sonny's hand and set it on the kitchen counter. Then she retrieved the blanket from his bed and covered him on the sofa. He turned to one side and mumbled something. She turned off the TV and the living room lamp. He shifted, but didn't wake.

In the dark she whispered, "What do you know about romance?"

The Vote to Decide Whether or Not Melvin Should Enlist (1943)

Dr. Lum	(A)	Melvin's father
Mrs. Lum	(A)	Melvin's mother
Phil Lum	(A)	Melvin's brother
Esther Hsieh	(F*)	Melvin's wife
Yang Wong Kar	(A)	Melvin's uncle
Yang Sun Lau	(A)	Melvin's aunt
Steven Yang	(A)	Melvin's cousin
Doug Yang	(A*)	Melvin's cousin
Nancy Yang	(A)	Melvin's cousin
Hsieh Fan Lo	(A)	Melvin's father-in-law
Hsieh Ming Jou	(A)	Melvin's mother-in-law
Melvin Lum	(F**)	

$$F = 2$$
$$A = 10$$

Total Number of Ballots = 12

(F) = For Melvin's enlistment.

(A) = Against Melvin's enlistment.

(F*) = Officially for, but was truly against because voter believed her husband's desire to enlist was inspired by the cartoon character Popeye.

(A*) = Officially against after voter's parents, Wong Kar and Sun Lau, threatened to send him to an orphanage, but was truly for based on voter's argument that "We [the U.S. Army] need to kick their [the Japanese's] asses out of our country [China]."

(F**) = Melvin's vote did not officially count in the final tallying, as decreed by Dr. Lum.

Building Airplanes That Can't Fly
(1942–1944)

The first time Esther met Melvin, her father had brought him home for dinner.

"Friend of yours?" she asked.

"Sure." Her father tapped Melvin on the back. "Go on into the kitchen."

"There are only three table settings," she said, and Melvin paused.

"Keep going, boy," her father said and Melvin went. "Then make one more setting," he told her.

That night Melvin hardly said a word as her father praised his skills in soccer ("a terrific striker") and his high marks in English and history. He'd just graduated from high school and was now working with his father at the local meat cannery.

She didn't realize until after Melvin left that this had been her first date with him. More specifically, she didn't realize that until after Melvin had left and her father asked, "How'd you like your first date with Melvin?"

The following evening, her father asked her to have a second date with Melvin. Just the two of them. Eat noodles. Chitchat. Stroll through Golden Gate Park. Romantic. "Melvin's a good boy," he said. "Honest. Strong body. And I promised his father years ago you'd marry him."

"That's your problem," she said.

"At least give him a second date. If you decide afterward you don't like him, you can say no." He pleaded with her for a week until she agreed.

On her second date with Melvin she sat him down in her kitchen and asked, "Have you had any previous experiences with women?" She didn't want a man who, at nineteen, had already dipped his chopsticks in many different bowls.

"I talk to my mother a lot," he said.

"That's not what I mean."

He smiled. "No, I've never visited the whorehouses."

"Do you like staying at home?" she asked.

"Sure."

"You like talking to your mother?"

"She's a smart woman, much smarter than me. She told me that in a drawer of sharp knives, I am not the sharpest one. She said I'm more like a spoon than a knife." He laughed at that, and Esther laughed.

Humility and awareness of one's limitations were nice qualities. He had a sense of humor, too. And he had the most beautiful shoulders she'd ever seen on a man. They were broad and well defined.

This, to her, was how finding a husband worked. You looked for a man with a strong, healthy body, and when you found him, you married him and the two of you raised kids and spent your old age rocking on chairs and listening to birds sing outside.

They married three months later and moved into his parents' home.

A month after their marriage, Melvin took her to Stan Chin's Chinatown Theater, located in the two-story apartment building

Stan Chin owned. It wasn't their first time attending the theater, but it was their first time seeing Popeye.

The interior walls on the second floor of the building had been knocked out to create one large room. A film projector, screen, and two hundred wooden chairs had been brought in, and every Saturday people bought tickets to see the features and shorts being shown in the rest of America beyond the Chinatown borders.

There were two main showings, one in the afternoon and one in the evening; Melvin loved the movies and liked to go to both. The evening shows offered live translations for those who didn't understand English. Stan Chin's wife, Amelia, would stand next to the projector and shout out in Cantonese what was happening.

"The little black kid's name is Buckwheat," she'd say. "'Otay' is African for 'It's a nice day.'"

In Amelia's translation, Abbott and Costello became Skinny and Fatty. "Fatty is giving Skinny a hard time for not eating enough. They're running away from Frankosteen the monster because he threatened to strangle them." Sometimes she'd editorialize. Of the Hindenburg disaster, she said, "See? This is what happens when rich people show off with big things. They die."

While the films ran, Stan Chin's grandfather was stationed outside the bathroom located in the main hallway on the first floor. He sat on a small wooden stool in a white T-shirt and pajama bottom, a pipe in his hand. Next to his feet was a lime green coffee mug with a piece of paper taped to it. On the paper was written the word TIPS.

As the theater's bathroom valet, his job was to say, "Hey, wash your hands when you're done," each time somebody entered. He also said, "There's someone in there. I said there's someone in there." Because indoor plumbing was a new experience for many of the theatergoers, some of whom would admire the sink and toilet for fifteen to twenty minutes, Stan Chin's grandfather would occasionally knock on the door and say, "No loitering. Not a museum in there."

The theater's customers deposited only cigarette butts, candy wrappers, and ticket stubs in the tips mug, which prompted Stan Chin to place next to his father two large cardboard signs. One was in English and the other in Chinese. They read:

Tipping the bathroom valet (with Cash Money) is an understood tradition in this country. For those who are new to these shores, I welcome you to participate in this fulfilling custom. For those who have been here for a while, you should know better.

There is a myth going around that Chinese businesses involved in the service industry (like restaurants and theaters) aren't accustomed to accepting cash money tips. This is a myth only, and was probably started by Chinese people who didn't want to tip.

Would you continue to deprive this cheerful old man of his only form of income?

Stan Chin's Chinatown Theater appreciates your continued support.

People began tipping with cash money, and Stan Chin put up another pair of signs:

Thank you for your enthusiastic support of the bathroom valet. Please note the ceramic jar next to him, which has been filled with lollipops and caramel squares. Please feel free to take one as a sign of our appreciation for your business. Please also show your fellow theatergoers consideration by not taking all you can fit into your pockets.

Stan Chin's Chinatown Theater appreciates your continued support.

It was at this theater, exactly one month after their marriage, that Esther and Melvin saw a matinee showing of Popeye cartoons.

You're a Sap, Mr. Jap had Popeye encountering a couple of Japanese fishermen who appeared peaceful but were actually hiding a larger warship, and *Spinach for Britain* showed Popeye delivering the green stuff to the English while a German submarine tried to stop him.

Popeye was a violent and unintelligent thug whose vegetable-derived superhuman strength enabled him to pummel enemies and friends alike.

He beat up on Nazis, that's one thing. But what about the times he dragged Olive Oyl around like a sack of rice? What about the times he "accidentally" knocked her about with his large, clumsy arms? What kind of a man knocked his girlfriend around? What kind of a woman stood by a man like that?

In the dark of the theater, Esther glanced at her husband and was disappointed to find him enthralled. His mouth hung slightly open and his eyes glimmered, reflecting the light of the screen.

When he came home several days later and showed her a tattoo of Popeye on his right biceps, she was horrified. If he saw himself as Popeye, then he probably saw her as Olive Oyl, a warbling bird whose willingness to be with someone like Popeye suggested a severe lack of self-respect.

"I have to look at that for the rest of my life," she said. "Or yours."

"It's pretty good," Melvin said. "It looks just like him."

That night in bed, he reached for her and started to unbutton her pajama top. She pushed his hand off her chest. Even though it was dark, she knew Popeye was gawking at her, waiting for her clothes to come off.

"What's wrong with you?" he asked.

"Get out of bed," she said. "Come on."

She moved carefully through the hallway, testing the hardwood floor with her toes before settling her full weight down to avoid loud creaks that would wake his parents and his older brother, Phil, whose room sat between hers and her in-laws'.

Esther turned on the living room lamp and found her mother-in-law's sewing supplies stuffed in a tin canister. "Come here." She measured the circumference of his biceps.

"You're making me a shirt?"

She sat and cut a long swatch of white cloth from leftover fabric.

"I don't think you can make a shirt in one night." He tickled her feet. She brushed his hand away. She wrapped his biceps with the cloth and bound it with two pieces of string. He looked like he'd suffered a major laceration, but it was better than having Popeye look at her while they were making love.

She touched the fabric, then ran her fingers from his shoulder down to his forearm, feeling the transition from flesh to cloth to flesh.

"Let's go." She turned off the lamp.

"Do I have to keep this on?" He took her hand and let her guide them back to their room at the end of the hall.

"Yes."

"Do I have to wear it whenever we do it?"

"Yes."

"You can't even see it in the dark," he said.

"Moonlight through our curtains."

"I yam what I yam," he whispered as they passed his parents' door.

"What did you say?" She made a sharp stop and he bumped into her.

"Shh. Lower your voice."

"Don't ever say that again." She gave his hand a hard squeeze.

"I was joking."

"Don't ever quote him," she said.

"Fine. Let's go."

The moon shone through their thin bedroom curtains as it did every night. She imagined that the right arm grazing her face and breasts was just temporarily injured. The bandages were covering a wound, and when unwound would reveal his arm as it'd always been, thin, pale, sparsely downed with hair, and free of defacement.

As he sloughed off his underwear and climbed on top of her, she was filled with neither excitement nor affection, both of which she'd felt intensely the first time she saw his penis, erect, curved skyward as if to say, "Nice to meet you."

Now all she could hear it saying was, I yam what I yam.

Six months after their marriage Melvin wanted to leave. "I have a duty to my country," he said.

"What do you mean by duty to your country?" she asked.

"I mean freeing the world from the fascist grips of Adolf, Mussolini, and Hirohito."

"And what do you mean by freeing the world from their fascist grips?"

"I mean going over there with a machine gun and liberating conquered villages."

"You sound like a cartoon." What Esther was digging at, what she knew he'd never admit, was that he'd been inspired to enlist by Popeye.

"You're my wife," he said, "which means you're my partner. Partners support each other."

"Not when one partner is making a bad decision."

"You should support me without exception," he said.

"If I supported you, we'd both be stupid."

"I'll come back," he said.

"If you don't get killed."

"I won't get killed."

"Don't leave."

They repeated this exchange for days until she realized he'd already made up his mind. She agreed to support his decision because he'd leave with or without her consent, and she wanted him to leave on good terms. She wanted to show only kindness and support so that if he later found himself injured on the battlefield, blood draining from his head and out of the various wounds on his body, he'd remember his kind and supportive wife and suffer even more pain at the thought of who he'd left behind, and who he could have spent a life with.

She told herself his departure would only be temporary. Supporting his decision in front of the family, that would be a permanent mark of her devotion to him, something the two of them would always remember as her love.

And he'd owe her for her love. If in the future she said, "Let's vacation in Mexico," and he was reluctant, she could say,

"You've already forgotten when I supported you in your decision to go to war, when your entire family was against you?"

But the idea of his indebtedness to her didn't make her feel better because she already started to miss him, and his being present when she tried to steel herself for his departure only caused her more frustration. "Go to another room," she'd say if they were both in the living room.

"What for?" he'd ask.

"I'm trying to picture your face in my mind. I can't do it if your face is right in front of me."

"Why are you trying to picture my face in your mind?"

"Go."

The entire Lum family, along with Esther's parents, officially assembled for the first time to discuss something other than a wedding or a meal. They sat in a circle in the Lums' living room and waited for Melvin to speak.

Dr. Lum coughed. Mrs. Lum looked anxious. Melvin's aunt and uncle whispered in each other's ears. Melvin's cousin Doug flicked his sister's earlobes. She slapped at Doug's hands. Esther's parents sat straight and looked stoic. Esther watched, her hands on her lap.

Melvin took a deep breath, then said, "I'm going to enlist in the army."

"The U.S. one?" Dr. Lum asked.

"No, the German one."

"Don't be smart with me, boy," Dr. Lum said. "I'll knock your head off and throw it into the bay before you can say another smart thing. I asked about the U.S. Army because didn't it occur to you, smart boy, that the U.S. doesn't even like you?"

"That's right." Mrs. Lum held up her copy of the December 1941 issue of *Life* magazine, which she kept taped open to the article "How to Tell Japs from the Chinese." She kept the magazine close as a constant reminder to her husband and children that the U.S. distrusted and disliked their kind, their kind being nonwhite.

"They're saying we're the good ones," Melvin said. He pointed to the head shots of Ong Wen-hao and Hideki Tojo, anthropological representatives of the Chinese and Japanese races, respectively. Perpendicular lines crisscrossed their faces and notes pointed out Ong's "more frequent epicanthic fold" and Tojo's "massive cheeks and jawbone."

Ong had a "parchment yellow and delicately boned" face whereas Tojo, the war-mongering Jap, was cursed with "yellow-ocher skin" and a "pug nose."

"Parchment is an ancient Greek city, a flat piece of animal skin used for writing, or an academic diploma," Melvin said. "Ocher is an earthy mineral oxide, like sand and dirt."

"Parchment?" Mrs. Lum asked. "Boy, your face is covered with acne."

"A son should always be handsome in his mother's eyes," Melvin said.

"You don't have parchment for skin," Mrs. Lum said. "And don't try to teach me English." Mrs. Lum taught English in an elementary school three blocks from their home.

"You don't have animal skin on your face, either," Dr. Lum said. "What kind of people would say you have animal skin on your face?"

"They mean an academic diploma," Melvin said. "They're saying we're not dirt."

Doug stopped flicking his sister's earlobes to say, "That

sounds like a good thing." His mother slapped him on the back of the head and told him to shut up.

Mrs. Lum slapped her own forehead in frustration. "If the white people in this country need a magazine to tell them that you're not a dirt-faced, ugly, pug-nosed son of a bitch, then they're not people you want to fight for in a war," she said.

Melvin said he had an obligation to help kick the Japanese out of China.

"You have no investment in China," Dr. Lum said. "You've never even been there. To have the right to fight for a country, you have to have set foot on its soil at least once."

"Then I have an obligation to fight the Japanese who attacked Pearl Harbor."

"You've never been to Hawaii," Dr. Lum said.

"Hawaii's part of the U.S," Melvin said.

"It's not," Dr. Lum said. "It's like Hong Kong. It's a colony."

"Tyrone Power's the most famous actor in this country," Melvin said. "He was born in Hawaii, which makes it part of our country." Melvin didn't think Tyrone Power was born in Hawaii, but his parents didn't know who the man was, so they didn't argue this claim.

Dr. Lum asked for a better reason for enlisting and Melvin said he wanted to help defeat the Nazis, Japanese, and Italians with a weapon begot of his Chinese heritage.

"Courage?" Melvin's brother Phil asked.

"The machine gun," Melvin said.

"The Chinese didn't invent the machine gun," Phil said.

"We invented gunpowder and there's no machine gun without gunpowder." By "we," Melvin meant not just the inventor(s) of gunpowder, but the entire Chinese brotherhood that had spread across time and space immemorial.

145

"In raising you, did we ever mention you should sign up for the opportunity to get a bullet slammed through your brain?" Mrs. Lum asked. "Have you been watching those Popeye cartoons again? Just because Popeye can beat up Nazis doesn't mean you can. He's a cartoon, child."

"Let the Europeans take care of it," Dr. Lum said. "Not our business."

"It is," Melvin said.

"Let the French deal with this mess," Mrs. Lum said.

"They didn't start the war," Melvin said.

"They could have stopped it by building something better than the Maginot Line," Dr. Lum said. "Built a wall of cannons to protect themselves, but didn't bother to extend it to the Belgian border. That's a whole country, Belgium. That's like saying, 'We're going to build a Great Wall,' and then building half a Great Wall instead. What kind of country builds half a Great Wall to protect itself? That's like building airplanes that can't fly."

"Don't be stubborn," Mrs. Lum said. "A man has to know when to stay away from a war, which is all the time. Don't be the Maginot Line."

"What does stubbornness have to do with the Maginot Line?" Melvin asked.

"What about the Japs?" Doug asked.

"Damn Japs," the convened Lums said. "Damn Japs."

"Damn Japs or no," Dr. Lum said, "Melvin's staying home."

They looked at Esther. "You're his wife," Mrs. Lum said. "Don't you want him to stay? You want to chance being a window?"

Esther's father said to Dr. Lum, "Your son cannot leave. I didn't give my daughter to a man who would be foolish enough to run off to war. I could have picked any husband for her. Any. Do you know how many suitors there were?"

146

Dr. Lum knew. All the Lums knew because her father would never let them forget how lucky they were to have one of their sons marry a Chinese girl who was neither a whore nor a divorcee, a young, unspoiled girl in a time when the Chinese men still outnumbered their women greatly, a girl whom approximately one hundred and twenty Chinese bachelors had courted.

"One hundred and twenty," her father said, and Dr. Lum nodded because he never had a response to that. "You're a foolish mule with shit for brains," her father said to Melvin. Dr. Lum winced, but said nothing.

Esther felt an impulse to defend her husband, but her father was right. Melvin was unwilling to move forward, backward, or sideways. He'd hold his ground even if it was breaking under his feet and the sea itself was threatening to burst through the cracks and drown him.

"I could have picked any of the other hundred and nineteen men," her father said to Dr. Lum. "But you promised me he'd be good to her, and now he's leaving after six months of marriage. That's a slap in my daughter's face. That says to me he's not happy with her and prefers the company of a group of soldiers to the most beautiful Chinese girl ever to walk the streets of San Francisco."

Dr. Lum waited for her father to finish, then looked at Melvin and said, "Reconsider."

Esther wanted to say to Melvin, Listen to these people, you mule. Listen. She looked at him, and he nodded at her to keep quiet.

"If you get shot, that's it," Dr. Lum said.

"Don't say that," Mrs. Lum said.

"I'm just saying."

"Don't."

"Okay," Dr. Lum said. "But my gun's not loaded anymore. You know what I'm saying? I'm dry. Out of bullets."

"I get it," Melvin said.

"No longer fertile," Dr. Lum said. "If you die, I lose half my offspring."

"I understand," Melvin said.

"The gun has no bullets."

"I said I understand."

"You don't. Because if you did, you'd understand that you're worth much to many people, and worth more than being a soldier. Nobody here wants you to enlist." Dr. Lum indicated the rest of the Lums, who echoed his sentiments:

"The old man's gun is dry."

"No more bullets."

"War's a game you can't win. Don't play."

"Damn Japs."

Melvin promised to rethink his decision that night.

He enlisted the next morning.

He shipped out fifteen days later.

The family reconvened the day after Melvin's departure to talk about what a stupid decision he'd made. They discussed ideas for bringing him home. They talked about sending someone overseas to drug him and carry his unconscious body back in a large plastic bag equipped with air holes. Esther's father suggested sending Phil because he was a chemist and knew what chemicals would work best at putting someone to sleep for a long time. Phil would have to travel overseas, of course, and find his brother in France. Phil declined to accept the mission.

They talked about sending a beautiful Chinese girl to seduce him and lure him home, until someone noticed Esther sitting in the corner of the room, looking very angry.

They talked about sending someone to stab him in the leg so he could get discharged. No one volunteered for this plan. No one liked the idea of getting blood on his hands.

They talked about sneaking into heavily fortified U.S. military bases, about plans that had no way of working logically or even in the wildest of dreams. They cooked up these ideas because if they didn't, they'd have nothing to talk about. Esther missed him more while listening to this foolishness.

"This is a day to remember Melvin," Dr. Lum said. "This day next year, if he's not home by then, we'll meet again to talk about what a fool he is."

"Cheers to that," her father said.

The apartment Esther shared with Dr., Mrs., and Phil Lum fell quiet. They wandered their home as if they were haunting it, the occasional tapping of feet against floorboards, the wood creaking. They spoke simple phrases. "Thank you for dinner." "Enough salt?" "Salt perfect." "Good." "Thank you again." "You're welcome." "Another letter from Melvin?" "He's safe?" "Good." They saw each other only at meals, and kept to themselves at all other times.

In silence Esther found the words of her discontent. Dr. and Mrs. Lum had failed the first law of parenting: If there is a war, do not under any circumstance allow your child to participate.

Their failure Esther believed in with more conviction than Melvin's safe return. She believed they had failed as parents. They should have taken action. They were the heads of the family. They should have argued against him until he changed his mind. She'd done the best she could to talk him out of it. They should have done more.

Nights, she lay awake and wondered if her in-laws were having sex two rooms away, and she felt jealous for the sex they might have been having. She wondered if she'd have sex when she was their age. She wondered if her in-laws rubbed against each other until the skin on their thighs and arms turned red, if they bruised each other's ribs and chests with their knees and elbows, if they bit each other.

She had a hard time conjuring Melvin's face because she couldn't hear his voice. Some nights she'd sit in the living room with the lights off. Sometimes Phil would come out of his room and join her in the dark.

"I'm just thinking," she'd say.

"That's fine." He never asked what she was thinking. He respected her privacy and she respected him for that.

He'd turn on the lights and offer to make tea. He rarely talked. He'd wait by the fire until the water boiled, and then pour the water into two cups and drop in the green leaves. He'd bring her a cup, serving her before himself. "Here, sister," he'd say.

Though he was only one of several assistants to the researcher who worked on diphenhydramine hydrochloride, she preferred to see him as the sole force behind its invention, which had been written about in one of the medical journals he liked to read after dinner. She felt such a kind man deserved the invention all to himself.

The family met again in '44 to discuss Melvin's foolishness. No one mentioned plans for getting him home this time. Instead they said he was a moron to go overseas when he had such a lovely wife at home, at which point Esther stood and said, "Please leave my name out of your mouths when you're insulting my husband."

Mrs. Lum spoke of the things Melvin used to do for her. "I used to have these painful cramps. He'd sit right there and massage my heels for fifteen, twenty minutes."

Dr. Lum talked about Melvin's love and courage, words that could mean everything and anything and so meant nothing to Esther, at least nothing regarding the Melvin she knew.

Phil stood and read a poem he'd written over the past year:

> **My Brother Melvin**
> Melvin,
> I look around,
> But you're not here.
> You left some time ago.
> You're over there.
> In France I mean.
> Can it be true?

The reading was followed by scattered applause and puzzled looks from Dr. and Mrs. Lum. "You write poetry?" Dr. Lum asked.

Months later, the family received word that Melvin had been killed in combat. Esther stayed in her room for two days, refusing to eat or talk. During this time, Mrs. Lum cried loudly in her own room, the sound of sobbing and sniffling passing through Phil's room and into hers. Esther wasn't a loud crier. She'd never made much noise as a child, but now felt she should answer her mother-in-law's anguish with a louder expression of anguish. Tears streamed down her face, but she didn't make a sound. No wailing, no moaning. That's fine, she thought, so I'm not loud.

Mrs. Lum, normally a nonpracticing Buddhist, asked Dr. Lum to construct a miniature shrine for Melvin. It consisted of a wooden board that stood upright from the wooden base to which it'd been nailed. She put it in the center of the living room floor and taped to the upright board a photo of Melvin, in front of which she placed a basket of apples, oranges, and bananas, and a clear glass vase filled with red sticks of incense that covered the home in the pine scent of grief. Each evening she and her husband kneeled in front of Melvin's photo, bowing and praying for his peace and happiness in the afterlife.

What was the point, Esther thought. He was gone. There was nothing left, nothing here or in an afterlife that didn't exist. There was only time and waiting for his body to be shipped home.

Phil wrote another poem and placed it alongside his brother's photo.

It read:

> **No More Fishing, Melvin**
> Melvin,
> We got the news
> Yesterday afternoon.
> We cannot go
> Fishing together anymore.
> I don't know
> What to say.

A week after the news of Melvin's death, the family discovered that it was Mark Ling from three blocks down who'd actually been killed. Mrs. Lum took down the shrine and Phil wrote yet another poem:

> **You're Alive, Melvin!**
> Melvin,
> The army clerk
> Made a mistake and sent the

Wrong telegram!
Thank goodness
You're alive!
Come home soon.

Esther wanted him to return soon, too, but she wanted back the man who'd left, not a stranger. She wanted wide-faced, skinny-nosed Melvin, and in her nightmares he came back changed, his face thinner, his chin elongated. Up close she could see the frequent epicanthic folds newly formed above his eyes, the folds she didn't want him to have because he'd looked perfectly natural and fine without them.

He must have yearned for these folds each night before he fell asleep, hoping their appearance would make his eyes more attractive and distinguish him from the enemy Japs, these folds *Life* had presented on the face of its friend and partner.

The Tragedy of Delicious Turnip Cakes (2002)

After taking off from LAX, Louis swallowed three Benadryl tablets and fell asleep. He had the recurring dream.

They were in Grandma Esther's beige dining room eating her fried turnip cakes and talking. He knew it was a dream because her turnip cakes tasted good, good not from hunger, but well cooked and perfectly seasoned, and stuffed with minced onions and shrimps.

The whole family was there, eating and talking. Connie was chewing on sunflower seeds. Will, training for football, talked about his biceps. "They grew three millimeters in the last week," he said. "Go ahead. Poke them. Like steel."

"Eat," Grandpa Melvin said. "Eat," Grandma said, and everybody ate because the turnip cakes actually tasted good.

Uncle Larry talked about the low rate on his refinance and Mick responded, "You think that's a low rate?"

Aunt Helen asked Uncle Bo and Aunt Julie about property values in Hong Kong.

His father Sonny was there.

His mother Mirla. "Your father has been driving you crazy, hasn't he?" she asked.

"Yes," Louis said. "Crazy."

Then things changed.

A soft yellow light sparked in the center of the ceiling and grew in intensity, threatening to consume the room.

The diphenhydramine hydrochloride Granduncle Phil had created contained two phenyl rings and a chain comprising the essential life ingredients of carbon, hydrogen, and nitrogen, which could be rearranged into the gas that Grandpa had ignited to fire the .30-caliber rounds that pierced the bodies of the German soldiers he'd confronted.

What went around came around.

Light covered the room, filled it, heated it. The light was so bright it hummed and pulsated, sending shock waves that shook the hairs on the back of Louis's neck. The light melted skin.

Connie's hands turned into running wax and the skin slid off her bones. Connie, twelve years old, asked, "Where am I going?"

"I don't know."

The skin on Will's steely biceps melted and left behind red muscle threaded with veins and arteries that also melted.

"Don't go."

Grandpa.

Uncle Larry.

Aunt Julie.

Skin, muscles, and bones dissolved to reveal molecules: hundreds of glowing green and red balls connected by clear tubes, like those three-dimensional plastic models Louis had studied with in college chemistry.

His mother melted like the rest, leaving behind green and red clusters that exploded, each glowing particle shooting through the walls of the dining room and trailing streaks of light.

The dead Lums had died again, and Grandma, Dad, Mick, Aunt Helen, Uncle Bo, and Louis were left at the table with six empty chairs.

"What happened?" Grandma asked.

A Really Strong Iron Gate
(2002)

The Grand Park Hotel rose eighty-five flights above the street bustle of Hong Kong's Tsim Sha Tsui District.

The green marble floor in the lobby sparkled. The male clerks wore black jackets and ties and the female clerks wore gray dresses. They all had on plastic pins that showed in vacuum-metallized silver the hotel's name.

In the center of the lobby was a brass fountain flanked by mermaids made out of plaster.

Beyond the mermaids was a long check-in counter on which sat a pineapple-shaped glass jar that held the hotel's personalized matchbooks. Louis took one, then another and another. He studied his reflections on the many-sided jar. He smiled at a female clerk. She looked at the matchbooks in his hands and frowned.

This was much nicer than the last hotel Louis had stayed in, the Holiday Inn. The Hong Kong Holiday Inn had been an option, but he wanted a genuine Hong Kong hotel, not a chain, not an import, not anything that bore the mark of the place he'd just come from. He wanted a hotel with a brass fountain and plaster mermaids.

The bellboy, a cap perched on top of his head, loaded Louis's luggage onto a cart. He asked in English, "Is there a problem?"

Louis pointed at a mermaid. "That's wonderful. What do you call it?"

"Statue in the lobby."

Louis followed the bellboy toward the elevators.

As they ascended, Louis said in Cantonese, "I can speak Cantonese."

The bellboy was staring at his feet. "Super."

"What's your name?" Louis asked.

"Aaron."

"Your real name," Louis said.

"What?"

"Your Chinese name," Louis said.

"Fu Sing."

Most people in Hong Kong had both an English and Chinese name. Learning the Chinese one made Louis feel like less of a tourist. "Beneficial meeting you, Fu Sing," he said.

"Your tones are wrong," Fu Sing said in English.

Louis's room was on the thirty-second floor. Fu Sing rolled Louis's luggage in and set it down next to his bed.

"They're all wrong?" Louis asked in English.

"Fifty percent. Sixty-five." Fu Sing looked sixteen, a tall, stocky kid whose thick neck strained his shirt collar.

Louis tipped him two Hong Kong twenty-dollar bills.

"Do you think people will understand me here?" Louis asked.

"Say something in Cantonese," Fu Sing said.

Louis said something.

"Your old bean lives in California?" Fu Sing asked.

"Old man."

"You're saying old bean instead of old man."

Fu Sing said old man in Cantonese, slowly and clearly like an instructor, and Louis repeated.

"That's better," Fu Sing said.

"I'll be able to walk here?" Louis asked in Cantonese.

"You have problems walking?"

"Place orders for restaurants. Discover how to navigate directions. You think people will comprehend me?"

Fu Sing looked puzzled.

"Do you think I speak well enough to find my way around here?" Louis asked in English.

Fu Sing took off his cap and ran his fingers through his hair. He flicked his wrist, fanning the sweat off his hand as he headed for the door. "Sure. If you speak English."

Louis called his father. "I've arrived, old bean," he said in Cantonese.

"Good. Have a fun vacation."

"I called you old bean instead of old man," Louis said in English.

"Okay."

"You didn't know that?" Louis asked.

"I've always known." His father yawned. It was four in the morning in Orange County.

"Why didn't you correct me?" Louis asked.

"Your mother thought it was cute."

"You should have corrected me."

"Say hi to Uncle Bo for me. Don't lose your wallet."

"I'll call you again before my flight home," Louis said.

"I'll talk to you then."

Louis hung up and looked out the window. High-rises cluttered the landscape. The narrow streets were jammed with red taxis.

He checked his wallet to see how many bills were left. A *man* is a dollar. A *man* is also a mosquito. Hundreds of people covered the sidewalks below like *man*.

Louis had a habit of mixing Cantonese and English when he spoke with his family. The problem with mixing languages was it was too convenient, it encouraged ignorance, and it encouraged not flipping through a Cantonese-English dictionary when the need arose.

When he'd wanted to say, "Old man, I need you to sign a permission slip so I can go on a field trip to the Griffith Observatory," he'd used English for every word except old man, I, you, sign, and go. He'd used English for scientific and technical words like electrons, power saw, and dual overhead camshaft. He'd used English to curse, or when he wanted to get a point across to his father in a loud way without raising his voice, as in, She's not a fucking leg.

He could understand them when he heard them, but the correct tones didn't transfer from the reception to the production areas of his brain. The number of words he could comprehend far outnumbered the ones he could recall and use at will. He could listen to Cantonese. He just couldn't speak it correctly.

The first two days Louis wandered the streets around his hotel, rode the subway, and hailed a couple of taxis, asking the drivers to take him to the "best place to eat in the area." The first driver dropped him off at a KFC, and Louis told the second driver, "A Chinese restaurant."

The third day Louis began searching for his uncle. He headed north on Chatham Road, moving forward with the flow of human traffic, constantly adjusting his shoulders and hips to avoid head-on collisions with oncoming pedestrians.

The burst of car horns and voices filled the street. The air was hot and humid, and a layer of moisture covered his arms and legs. At some point, his uncle's feet must have touched this pavement, his eyes must have scoured the high-rises above, and his nose must have picked up the scent of barbecued duck hanging from miniature gallows behind restaurant windows.

Gai. Live chicken cackling in an alleyway, the birds held in square wooden boxes with spaced slats along the sides.

Mah. Mother dragging her son through an intersection like he was a Labrador retriever, his left arm the leash.

Bouji. Newspaper in a newsstand holding news, anime magazines, comic books, and porn.

Gaai. Street.

Giu. Hail.

Diksi. Taxi.

Louis handed to the driver the sheet of paper with Uncle Bo's address on it. The flat was in Kowloon City northeast of Tsim Sha Tsui.

The driver looked Louis up and down. In this August heat, most of the young people were dressed in black jeans and tight black T-shirts. Louis had on a pair of sneakers and cargo shorts that covered his knees.

"*Ganahdaaihyahn?*" the driver asked. Canadian?

"*Meihgwokyahn. Gahjau.*" American. California.

"*Taam gatihng?*" Visiting family?

"*Haih.*" Yes.

"*Neih yauh gatihng hai Gahjau?*" You have family back in California?

"*Ah-bah.*" Father. Not old man and not old bean.

Louis paid the driver and stepped out of the taxi. In front of him loomed another tall building. It stood at the end of a quiet cul-de-sac like those found in Irvine and Mission Viejo. The structure resembled a stick of polished marble, very different from the government-sponsored ghettos he'd passed by on the way here, those concrete high-rises that housed hundreds of families.

Here an electrically powered wrought-iron gate sealed off the Paradise Plaza flats from the rest of Kowloon City. It had straight vertical bars that ended in spikes.

There was a com device with a numbered keypad in front of the gate. The number Louis dialed was the number of the flat Uncle Bo had rented a room in.

"*Wei?*" It was a woman's voice.

"My name is Louis Lum," he said in English slowly and clearly. "I am Bo Lum's nephew. Can you please let me in?"

There was a pause. Then she hung up.

Louis called again. "I am Bo's nephew. Please let me in."

"Please go home," she said.

"I can't. I'm already here."

A pause. He heard her breathing. A long pause followed by a click and the dial tone.

He called again. The answering machine came on. Her voice said in Cantonese, "We cannot come to the phone right now. Please leave a message. Thank you."

"This is Louis Lum," he said. "I'm staying here until you let me in." He disconnected and approached the gate. He kicked it, just to see whether it would give. The iron bar sang softly. He kicked it again harder. The bar whined a little louder and the gate shook slightly. Maybe it wasn't that tough. Maybe it only looked strong. He swung his hip and kicked hard as he could against the bar. The pain shot through his right foot and he let out a yell. He walked gingerly back to the com device. He sat and took off his shoe and sock. His big toe was throbbing, but not broken. He could still move it. He heard footsteps and quickly put his sock and shoe back on.

The woman pretended to inspect the hedges that lined the opposite side of the gate. The individual shrubs resembled jade mah-jongg tiles. They'd been meticulously trimmed.

"Who are you?" he asked.

She wore sunglasses.

"Who are you?" he asked again.

She turned the other way.

"I have to find Uncle Bo," Louis said. "Not finding him would kill my grandmother."

That stopped her. Louis tried Cantonese. "My grandmother would slice her own gizzard chancing I do not discover my uncle." The words weren't what he'd wanted to say, but he hoped the sentiment of desperation came through.

She hesitated, then pulled what looked like a garage opener from the left pocket of her jeans. She pushed a button. The electric motor purred and swung the gate open to reveal a path wide enough for two cars, one coming in, one going out. Louis took the path of the incoming car and followed her inside.

She introduced herself in English-accented English (she'd grown up in Leeds) as Lum Fei. Her husband, Wai, had left this morning with their son, Ah-Kai, to visit one of Wai's old university friends.

"Lum?"

"When he first moved here, your uncle looked up all the Lums in the telephone directory. He felt he could trust someone with the same name. He wanted to rent a room from a Lum. We were the fourth on his list."

Louis sat across the kitchen table from her. The walls were covered with framed artwork from Hong Kong martial arts comic books. Men with long robes and longer queues whirled in midair, brandishing swords and fists.

"Who drew this?" Louis asked.

"I did." Fei said she was an artist. She must have been a successful one. This flat was spacious for Hong Kong housing. It had a full kitchen, a large living room, and even a dining area.

"How was your flight?" she asked.

"I slept most of the way."

"You're lucky. I can't sleep when I'm flying."

"I took a lot of Benadryl," he said. "It's the antihistamine that makes you sleepy. My granduncle invented—"

She looked confused.

"Never mind," Louis said. "He's not here, is he?"

"That's what I told your grandmother. I told her she didn't need to worry." Fei rubbed the skin on her knuckles. The outer edge of her left hand, where it must have pressed against the pages as she drew, was stained with black ink. The inside of her middle finger was callused.

"Do you have pictures of him?" Louis asked.

"Yes. Of course." She went to her bedroom and returned with two photo albums. One was orange and the other red. She set them side by side and sat next to him. "Please, go ahead."

He opened the orange one first. He saw Uncle Bo arm wrestling Wai. Fei hummed in recognition as he flipped the pages, as though each picture sparked synapses in her brain, brought back familiar emotions (happiness? disappointment?) directly hardwired to these prints.

He saw Wai and Fei eating noodles. Fei and Aunt Julie sitting on the grass in front of a pond. Uncle Bo with his arm around Aunt Julie.

Fei nodded at the red album. "These are with Ah-Kai. He was born a year after Julie died."

Uncle Bo had stopped writing after Aunt Julie's death. The photos inside probably held intimate moments he'd wanted to keep to himself, far away from his family in California. Louis opened it eagerly.

There was Uncle Bo holding Ah-Kai in the delivery room, the baby wrapped in a cocoon of sheets. Uncle Bo and Fei standing next to Ah-Kai's crib. The boy standing on his own two feet and Uncle Bo towering over him, opening his mouth wide like he was going to eat him. Uncle Bo with Ah-Kai in front of the steel railing at Victoria Peak. Uncle Bo sitting next to Wai and Ah-Kai, their faces obscured by steam rising from their bowls of rice porridge.

His uncle's expressions ranged from uncomfortable to various degrees of pain. "He hated having his photo taken," Fei said. She looked at the kitchen. "Would you like some tea?"

"Sure."

While they drank, the front door opened and a man's voice said, "I'm home," in Cantonese. Wai came into the kitchen with Ah-Kai. If he was born a year after Aunt Julie died, then he was eight. He looked Louis over like the taxi driver had done, studying his sneakers and shorts. He was carrying a big red plastic robot. It was covered in a film of dirt and its left fist looked as if it'd been melted with a flamethrower. On its head were five spikes, one of which appeared to have been gnawed off.

"This is Bo's nephew," Fei said.

"Welcome." Wai shook Louis's hand.

"How are you doing?" Ah-Kai asked in his mother's accented English.

"Fine," Louis said. "That's an interesting toy."

"It's not for me," Ah-Kai said.

A long pause.

"So you were visiting your father's friend?" Louis asked.

"Yes," Ah-Kai said. He put the robot on the floor. Its head reached his stomach. "He gave this to me, no charge. I'm going to sell it to someone in Australia."

"That's a good investment," Louis said.

"What do you want from us?" Ah-Kai asked.

"Ah-Kai." Fei frowned at him, then looked at Louis. "He's very direct. Too much so."

"I'm looking for my uncle Bo."

"He was my uncle, too," Ah-Kai said.

"Let's go put the toy away," Wai said, and put a hand on Ah-Kai's shoulder.

"What happened to him?" Louis asked.

"Wait," Fei said.

Wai squeezed his son's shoulders, but couldn't stop the words from coming out.

"He died," Ah-Kai said.

Polyethylene Dreams
(2002)

Louis had expected Fei to tell him his uncle was in another part of Hong Kong. He had not expected to hear that Uncle Bo had fallen off a ferry into the harbor six months ago. He had not expected to hear that Uncle Bo had been fished out of the water bloated and blue. He deserved more from the man.

"Why didn't you tell my grandmother the truth?" Louis asked.

"She's already had two heart surgeries," Fei said. "I thought the news might kill her. She's had a hard life, raising Bo herself after your grandfather died in the war."

Grandma didn't tell him she'd lied to Fei. Grandma was in perfect health, healthier than the rest of the living Lums. "Yes, she's in bad shape," he said. "Where's my uncle?"

Per Uncle Bo's will, Fei had had him cremated and placed his ashes near Aunt Julie's in a memorial center in Mong Kok. Aunt Julie had picked this location because she'd wanted convenience for Uncle Bo. She'd wanted to be somewhere on the way between his work and the Lum's home. She hadn't wanted her ashes to be placed in Hong Kong Island, for example, because then he'd have to cross the harbor to see her. He'd have to pay a ferry or subway fare each time and the cost would have built up over the years.

"I want to see him," Louis said.

"We can get lunch first," Ah-Kai said.

"Good idea," Wai said.

Ah-Kai invited Louis to see his room, and Fei and Wai went to their room at the other end of the hall to discuss a location for lunch. They closed their door.

Ah-Kai seemed fine with the knowledge of Uncle Bo's death, as much as Louis was disturbed by it. He looked at Getter Dragun, the battered red robot Ah-Kai was planning to sell to a man in Australia.

"Who collects those things?" Louis asked. The toy was two feet tall and made of the same tough plastic as shampoo bottles.

Back in the seventies, Ah-Kai explained, a Japanese toy company began making Jumbo Machinders. Because these robots were so big, most of them got thrown out by parents. The ones that survived became collectible and (mostly) men from countries including Italy, France, the Philippines, and the United States were paying over four figures (U.S. dollars) for rare pieces in mint condition.

Getter Dragun was a relatively common Jumbo, and this one was in poor shape.

Ah-Kai had spent the last two years acquainting himself with his father's friends, schoolmates, and business associates, and anyone else who might have kept from childhood a Jumbo or two. He also visited antique toy stores nestled in alleyways and the top floors of multistory shopping plazas. Most of the Jumbos he'd sold had damaged or missing parts. Only a couple had been in near-mint condition. When he acquired a piece, he'd post sales ads on Japanese toy BBS's or auction it online.

"Your father never kept his?" Louis asked.

"He had one and I sold it a year ago," Ah-Kai said. "When I'm thirty I don't think I'll spend thousands on old toys."

"You might miss things you grew up with. You might want them back."

"Not toys."

Fei and Wai were still in their room, speaking in hushed voices. Louis stepped into the hall, but he couldn't make out their words from Ah-Kai's doorway. He walked back inside. "Your parents always take this long to discuss lunch?"

Ah-Kai shrugged.

"You don't collect anything?" Louis asked.

"Money," Ah-Kai said.

"What for?"

"Tuition." Ah-Kai planned to attend Hong Kong University, the best university in the territory. Even though his parents had offered to subsidize his education, he insisted on "tying his own shoelaces." He was already using his robot fund to pay for weekend cram classes and a tutor to ensure high marks in school.

"What do you want to study in college?" Louis asked.

"Business."

"What do you want to do after college?"

"Mergers and acquisitions."

"Neat," Louis said.

"What do you do?" Ah-Kai asked.

"I work at a magazine."

"You plan to work there for a long time?"

"I don't know," Louis said.

"You don't have any plans for the future?"

"To stay alive."

"Oh," Ah-Kai said.

Fei and Wai finished their conversation and came into Ah-Kai's room. Forty-five minutes had passed. "You two ready to go?" Fei asked.

Lunch was rice and three plates of stir-fried vegetables at a restaurant across the street from Fei's flat. They ate quickly and quietly, finishing in far less time than Fei and Wai had taken to figure out where to eat. Louis wondered what they'd been discussing about him.

Wai paid the bill and they got up to leave.

"Are you angry at him?" Fei asked.

Louis said nothing.

"Are you angry at me?" she asked.

"No," Louis said.

"Please don't be angry at your uncle."

Outside Wai hailed a taxi that took them to Mong Kok. The driver dropped them off in front of the memorial center.

Ah-Kai spotted an ice cream parlor across the street and asked to go. "We'll wait for you outside," Wai said to Fei, and crossed the street with his son.

"We told Ah-Kai where Bo's remains are, but he hasn't visited," Fei said.

"Does he want to?" Louis asked.

"No," she said. "I asked him about Bo and he said he doesn't feel as sad as he did six months ago. School and his toy business take up a lot of time. He'll probably start forgetting about Bo in another year." She sounded happy.

"Do drownings happen often in the harbor?"

"Not often," Fei said. "It was an unlikely accident."

"Unlikely things happen to my family."

"I know you're disappointed about him."

"I'm not disappointed," Louis said. "I'm angry."

"Why?"

"I wrote him a letter. He never wrote back."

"I'm sorry," she said.

The HappyLand Memorial Center was a gray stone building. Inside, life-sized statues of Mickey and Minnie Mouse flanked the front desk. Fei signed the pink guest list and led Louis deeper inside. There were colorful urns in the shapes of cartoon characters ranging from Japanese classics like Astro Boy and Doraemon to American standards like Woody Woodpecker and Snow White.

Fei led Louis through several aisles and past hundreds of urns before stopping in front of a bust of Green Lantern.

"I always liked Green Lantern," Fei said. "He has that really powerful ring."

Affixed to Green Lantern's chest was a bronze plaque on which Uncle Bo's name had been written in Chinese. Louis understood the character for Lum, but not the others.

"I never knew Uncle Bo's Chinese name." Louis touched the side of the urn with his fingers. Cold ceramic. "Where's Aunt Julie?"

Fei led him to another aisle. She pointed up at Hello Kitty.

Aunt Julie had wanted Uncle Bo to smile when he visited her. She'd thought that Hello Kitty was a character who, even in the form of an urn, would make him smile.

Louis wanted to have a quiet moment of solemnity, a moment in which to say something like I'm sorry you're dead, Uncle Bo.

Children were running through the aisles, pointing and shouting, "Look. Pluto! Bugs!"

"Let's get out of here," Louis said.

Outside Wai and Ah-Kai were waiting for them. They walked

along the street and Wai talked proudly of Fei's popularity and her talent, which Louis didn't doubt, having seen her colorful work on the walls of their home. Fei was the writer and artist of the comic book *Rose-Colored Fist*, in which martial arts superhero Cloud Bird traveled across fifteenth-century China attempting to master his qi, his fighting and life energy.

Fei walked up ahead and hailed a cab.

"Thanks for taking me to see him," Louis said. "My hotel's not far from here. I can walk back."

"Have dinner with us," Fei said.

"You've already shown me a lot of hospitality."

By the time Louis said, "No. Really. Thanks," Fei had pulled him into the backseat. Wai sat up front and Louis was stuck between Ah-Kai and Fei.

"We're much closer to my home than to Tsim Sha Tsui," Fei said. "You can spend the night with us. We'll take you back to your hotel tomorrow morning." She looked at him, but seemed to be thinking of something else. It was the way she'd looked at him all day, the absentiminded way his mother used to look at magazines, as if she was picturing herself driving the Mercedes down a country road instead of noticing the advertisement itself. "You can sleep on Ah-Kai's floor," Fei said.

"Fine with me," Ah-Kai said.

Louis wondered how he'd break the news to Grandma Esther. He thought about it the rest of the afternoon, through dinner, and while Fei placed a sheet and blanket on the floor next to Ah-Kai's bed. "You still look upset," she said.

"My uncle was a very irresponsible man," Louis said.

Fei looked disappointed.

"He was," Louis said.

*　　*　　*

He couldn't sleep. It was dark and he wasn't used to lying on the floor. He stared at the ceiling. He felt hot and kicked off his blanket. His chest and armpits were moist with sweat. His heart was pounding.

He was furious. The man should have left a note, should have called to say good-bye before he decided to give up his family and adopt another, before he drowned. It was about manners. Decency. Doing Things The Right Way.

"You're awake," Ah-Kai said.

"Sorry."

"Do you want to read something?" Ah-Kai got out of bed and turned on the lamp. "You think that'll help?"

"I'd like to see your mother's work," Louis said.

"Sure." There was a small bookshelf at the foot of Ah-Kai's bed. He pulled from it an issue of *Rose-Colored Fist* and handed it to Louis.

Ah-Kai translated as Louis turned the pages. They went through several issues. Almost every story involved Cloud Bird meeting strangers and challenging them to match his fighting technique, which they never could.

He'd beat them down with techniques that included the Rolling Rock Fist and the Boisterous Thunder Kick. After their defeats, the opponents would say, "Much respect, Cloud. Your qi is strong," before hobbling away on crutches.

Louis's eyes were getting tired and he felt ready to try sleeping again. "I'm done." He handed the issue he was looking at back to Ah-Kai and lay down on his blanket.

Ah-Kai looked around the room, then picked up the battered Getter Dragun robot he'd just received earlier that day and handed it to Louis. "Try sniffing it. The smell's interesting. It might help." Then he turned out the lights again.

173

The plastic used for shampoo bottles was polyethylene. Louis pulled the toy close and sniffed its neck. Decades ago, someone had cradled this thing with affection, had thrown it off rooftops and set it on fire, had brought it home cracked and broken, had kept it for the memories it held, had given it away. It smelled like Super Glue and gasoline.

He felt himself passing out, passing into a dream, that dream with the tasty turnip cakes, the Lums melting into molecules.

Steam was rising from the turnip cakes. The entire family was there. Everyone was talking and suddenly the room began shaking. No burning light. No melting skin. An earthquake instead. Louis thought they'd all die this time. He looked forward to not being left alone with Grandma asking, as she always did, what happened. But the earth wasn't quaking. His body was and the epicenter was in his right forearm. He grabbed it, squeezed it to stop it from shaking.

He woke and saw a hand around his wrist. He looked up and saw Fei. She put a finger to her lips.

The lights in Ah-Kai's room were still out and he was snoring softly. Louis followed her to the living room, then out the front door. The night air was warm and smelled of car exhaust.

"I called a taxi," she said. "It'll take you to your uncle."

"He's alive?"

Uncle Bo's phone number was all Fei had of his contact information. He'd given it to her with the understanding that she wouldn't call him. She'd called to say there was an emergency. He'd asked what the emergency was. She'd said Louis had arrived.

"He wouldn't have agreed to meet me so easily," Louis said.

"I spent an hour begging him to see you," she said. "I told him your grandmother had just had another open-heart surgery. I said she didn't have much time left and you were carrying a note from her."

They passed the iron gate and stopped in front of a waiting taxi. "Give us a few minutes," she said to the driver. She turned to Louis. "Before he left, your uncle spent a lot of time caring for Ah-Kai. He was a great help to us through those early years, changing diapers and feeding him, watching him so Wai and I could go out to dinner or a movie. He helped raise our son. So when he asked us not to give out contact information to his family, we honored his request. We felt we owed him."

"You make him sound like he's part of your family. You didn't have the right to withhold information from mine."

"We decided not to rent out his room again after he left," she said. "He was part of our family. I didn't want to lie to you at first, but when Ah-Kai told you he was dead, Wai and I had a long talk about whether or not to let you believe it.

"We thought if you believed he was dead, the knowledge would bring you peace like it did Ah-Kai. But when you held the urn, you looked so angry. I didn't want you to leave here hating Bo."

"The names on those urns?" Louis asked.

"Different Lums. No relation. We found them in case Ah-Kai decided to visit Bo."

The driver honked his horn. Fei ignored him. "After he married Julie, Bo moved out and found a place not far from ours. After Julie died, he asked us to leave him alone. For a year he wouldn't answer his phone or door. Then Ah-Kai was born and he moved back in with us. For a while the baby made him happier. When he told us he was leaving again, he said it would be permanent this time. We said Ah-Kai would be upset if he just disappeared. He said saying good-bye would make it harder on the boy."

175

"You lied to him," Louis said.

"We didn't want him to feel rejected by Bo. Ah-Kai won't have to wonder why he left, why he doesn't want to stay in touch. He'll know. Bo drowned in the harbor."

The driver honked again.

Fei turned to shout at him, but Louis stopped her. "I should go." He opened the taxi door.

"I hope he explains why he never wrote you back," she said.

Louis got in and shut the door.

"You finally done talking?" the driver asked.

Louis glared at him. "Get going."

The Genealogy of Bo
(1261–2002)

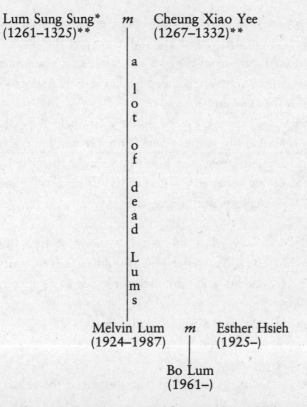

Lum Sung Sung*   *m*   Cheung Xiao Yee
(1261–1325)**   (1267–1332)**

a
l
o
t

o f

d
e
a
d

L
u
m
s

Melvin Lum   *m*   Esther Hsieh
(1924–1987)   (1925–)

Bo Lum
(1961–)

* = According to Bo, Lum Sung Sung's life was "indisputable fact." According to Louis, Lum Sung Sung was "indisputably a work of fiction."
** = Dates are approximate.

An Ideal Room
(2002)

Seated next to a window and lit by golden arches, Uncle Bo was playing with his fries. He was thinning, the hairs having begun a migration from the top and front of his head down to the sides, where they were slicked back. He wore a short-sleeved, button-down shirt and jeans.

The McDonald's near Fei's home was Uncle Bo's pick. He hadn't given Fei his address and probably wouldn't give it to Louis. He stared intently at his fries, using a thin hard one to prod the others softened by grease. Louis approached slowly, feeling both nervous and angry.

"Hi."

Uncle Bo's head shot up. After a moment, he stood and approached Louis, and patted his shoulders as if to verify their solidity. He was thin and tanned to the shade of a paper grocery bag. "Wow."

"You shouldn't be alive, Uncle Bo."

His uncle took a step back. "What?"

"Fei said you were dead."

"I see." His uncle smiled and motioned at the table. "You want some fries?"

"Not hungry," Louis said, and sat down across from his uncle. Despite the length of Uncle Bo's stay in Hong Kong,

178

he still spoke with a clear American accent. He looked worried.

"Grandma's never had heart surgery," Louis said. "She's in perfect health."

"She's not sick?"

"She'll probably outlive me."

Uncle Bo laughed, and when he noticed Louis's expression, stopped. "You're not carrying a note from her?"

"No," Louis said.

"Fei's a convincing liar," Uncle Bo said. "A very practical woman."

"You admire her lying?"

"Practical thinking is a necessity in life. You've met Ah-Kai, right? When he was a baby, he used to get a kick out of it when I'd raise him over my head. Up and down, up and down like a free-fall ride at an amusement park. He'd laugh and clap. The second I put him back on the ground, he'd start crying."

"And you'd pick him up again?"

"For the first year and a half, I'd hold him for hours at a stretch. Wai and Fei would be out on errands and I'd carry him around the flat to keep him quiet. I learned to cook and eat with one hand. Later I learned to let him cry. I'd put him back on the floor after playing with him. He'd scream and wail. His face would turn red. Big drops of tears would roll down his cheeks. I felt guilty, like I was traumatizing him. But he had to learn to stop crying."

"Did he?" Louis asked.

"I learned to stop playing with him."

"He believes you're dead."

"That's the best thing for him to believe."

"Why didn't you answer my letters?" Louis asked.

"Well."

Louis thought the well would preface an explanation and an apology, which would preface his forgiveness ("Even though you blew me off, I'll forgive you") that would then preface a conversation about what he'd been up to all these years, but Uncle Bo wiped his fingers with a napkin, leaned back in his chair, and seemed content with saying nothing else.

"What kind of a response is that?" Louis asked, his voice loud.

"Don't be upset. You're my favorite nephew."

"You never knew my cousins," Louis said. "Why didn't you write back?"

Uncle Bo glanced at the ceiling, then at the table.

"You could have let me know you weren't writing anymore," Louis said.

Uncle Bo opened his mouth as if to say something, then shut it again.

"Answer a simple question," Louis said.

"Don't shout at me."

"I'm not shouting!"

"Eat some fries!" Uncle Bo pushed his tray toward Louis. Louis pushed it off the table and the fries scattered on the ground.

Uncle Bo looked at the floor.

"Answer the question," Louis said.

A McDonald's employee came by. "The garbage can's over there. It's for garbage." He cleaned up the mess on the floor and shot a long stare at Louis as he walked away.

"You know what makes me happy?" Uncle Bo asked. "Single room. Heavy black curtains. A mattress on the floor and a thick comforter. Bottles of water. Tins of sardines. No phone. No television. Air conditioner set to high so I can cover myself head to toe in the comforter all day."

Louis wasn't sure how to respond to that. He wanted an answer to his question. Maybe this was his uncle's answer. This was some fucked-up answer.

Uncle Bo glanced at his watch.

"Am I keeping you up?" Louis asked. "Early day tomorrow?"

"I start work at three in the morning. I'm usually up this time of night. You're not keeping me up."

"I shouldn't have knocked the fries off the table," Louis said. "Made more work for that kid."

"Julie never yelled, hardly ever raised her voice."

"You want to talk about her?" Louis asked.

"Do you want to listen?"

"If you're not going to answer my question, I don't care what you talk about. I just need to bring Grandma proof you're alive."

Uncle Bo thought about it. "How's your father doing?"

"He's been driving me crazy."

"I'm sorry about your mother," Uncle Bo said.

"He's been a pain," Louis said.

"He can be a difficult man."

"I live with him now."

"That must be hard," Uncle Bo said.

"He can be irritating," Louis said.

Uncle Bo nodded.

"But I can't ignore him," Louis said. "And I don't understand why you'd ignore your mother. Make her cry."

"She's not the crying type."

"She wasn't before."

"She's a tough woman," Uncle Bo said.

"I don't understand why you can't return a damn form if all you have to do is check some boxes, especially when it comes with a self-addressed stamped envelope."

Uncle Bo was quiet.

"I'm going to order something to eat." Louis got up and walked to the row of registers. He placed his order with the boy who'd swept away the fries.

"If you can please keep this off the floor, I'd appreciate it." The boy slapped two cheeseburgers down on the tray.

Louis returned to the table. "Want one?"

Uncle Bo shook his head. "You said your father's been driving you crazy. How?"

"I didn't come here to talk about him."

"I'd like to know how he's doing," Uncle Bo said.

Louis looked at his food. "He wants to kill the guy who killed Mom."

"Do you want to kill him?"

"No," Louis said.

"I don't believe in violence, either."

"You also don't believe in responding to letters from relatives."

"I should have let you know I wasn't going to write any-more," Uncle Bo said. "Your grandmother—"

"Your mother," Louis said.

"My mother has a strong grip," Uncle Bo said. "I left for Berkeley when I was seventeen. My parents dropped me off at my dorm and she hugged me before leaving. About as strong as the bear hugs Sonny used to give me as a kid. He'd squeeze until it hurt to breathe. He'd leave bruises on my sides. She had that kind of a grip. She gave me that hug twice in my life. At Berkeley and before I left for Hong Kong."

"You're exaggerating," Louis said.

"No," Uncle Bo said. "Filling out those forms was like getting a bear hug from her. Every box I marked was a squeeze.

"After Julie passed away, I felt squeezed just being around people. I'd get frustrated with them because they were alive and Julie was dead. Even people I considered friends. I'd get mad at them for breathing and taking up space on the subway, on the bus, in my home."

"You want to talk about her?" Louis asked.

"My mother?"

"Aunt Julie."

"Let me think about it," Uncle Bo said.

Louis unwrapped one of the cheeseburgers and began eating. "The room you described, I've thought about it before. Something quiet and plain with no phone so I won't have to take any more calls from Dad. A place no one will think of visiting. San Bernardino. Bakersfield."

"You understand?" Uncle Bo asked.

"I wouldn't want to live in it permanently."

"I'm glad you've thought about it," Uncle Bo said.

Louis was considering the second cheeseburger.

"You're not hungry?" Uncle Bo asked.

"I'm not in the mood for fast food." Louis stood and tossed the burger into a garbage bin nearby. "I left my camera at the hotel. Come on. I need to take a photo of you."

"Are you still hungry, Louis?"

"Why?"

"I know a better place to eat," Uncle Bo said.

"Do they serve turnip cakes?"

They talked on the sidewalk, the subway, and all the way back to Tsim Sha Tsui, where Uncle Bo took them to an all-night café in an alleyway off Granville Road. It was the size of a living room, with six small square tables placed against each other in two rows. The café was full and people were chatting outside.

"It's worth the wait," Uncle Bo said.

Twenty minutes later, they were waved inside to a table right next to the cash register, which rumbled and rang loudly whenever a customer came up to pay.

Louis sat across from Uncle Bo, the two of them squeezed between other customers. The room was loud, warm, and filled with the aroma of hoisin sauce, bottles of which dotted the tabletops. The sauce was thick and had both a sweet and spicy flavor.

Uncle Bo ordered two bowls of rice porridge with pork and preserved egg, a plate of gai lan, and a plate of fried turnip cakes.

"You like that stuff?" Uncle Bo asked.

"Grandma makes it."

"I remember."

"I want to know what it should actually taste like," Louis said.

Uncle Bo smiled.

When the food arrived, Louis picked a piece of turnip cake with his chopsticks and held it in front of his nose.

"It smells funny?" Uncle Bo asked.

"No. I want to savor this."

The cake was studded with diced beef and green onions. It smelled wonderful and Louis put it in his mouth. The texture was soft on the inside but not flaccid, and tough on the outside but not hard. It'd been perfectly fried, not burnt, not under-cooked. It'd been prepared with discipline and devotion.

"Good?" Uncle Bo asked.

"I dream about this all the time. The dream doesn't come

close." He slurped porridge from his spoon, bit into the crisp stems of the gai lan, and listened while his uncle talked.

Uncle Bo mentioned that Julie had admired the shape of his head, which she'd thought resembled a duck egg. She'd held a deep affection for and kept the refrigerator stocked with cases of soy milk. They'd both been late eaters and sleepers. Dinner had started at nine and bedtime had been one in the morning. Sometimes she'd allow them to sleep feet to face so he could dream cuddling her butt. "It was nice," Uncle Bo said.

"Where do you work?" Louis asked.

"A bakery." Uncle Bo spoke of his satisfaction with his job. He was a baker and worked from three in the morning until the afternoon. "It's peaceful. Just me and the flour."

Louis talked about his job at the magazine, which was not as satisfying, but which paid a salary that had afforded a studio apartment and food.

Uncle Bo was surprised to hear that Louis's father was overweight, and happy to learn that Mick was lifting and in good shape.

The waitress dropped off the check.

"I'll get it," Uncle Bo said.

Louis looked at the empty plates. "The food was delicious."

"I'm sorry I didn't write back."

"Thanks for dinner," Louis said.

They shook hands in the lobby of the Grand Park Hotel.

"I'm glad you're not dead," Louis said.

"You can call Fei when you land. She'll let me know you've arrived home safely."

"I don't want to trouble her any further," Louis said.

"I'm sure you'll have no problems with your flight."

"I'll be fine."

"Take care." Uncle Bo turned to leave.

"I have to run up and grab my camera," Louis said. "Come with me."

"I'll wait down here," Uncle Bo said.

"You'll leave."

"I promise I'll be here."

"I don't trust you," Louis said.

"I'll be here. Hurry up and get the camera."

Louis took the elevator up, ran to his room, picked up the camera, and ran back to the elevator, thinking on the way down, He won't be there.

And he wasn't.

Louis searched the lobby, looking behind the mermaids and the fountain before the concierge tapped his shoulder and said his uncle was outside.

"Hey!" Uncle Bo called from across the street.

Cars buzzed by. Pedestrians filled the sidewalks.

"Take a long shot!" Uncle Bo waved for him to hurry up and take the picture.

Louis looked through the viewfinder. His uncle's face was covered in shadow. He lowered the camera. "I'll come across!"

"Do it from there!" Uncle Bo looked ready to run and Louis didn't want to chance having nothing.

"Move to your right. By that sign!" Louis waved him to a spot in front of a restaurant window. Uncle Bo stuffed his hands in his jeans pockets, eyes glancing left and right, mouth an even line. The restaurant's white neon lights lit him from above. Taped to the window was a sign that read in big black letters:

ROASTED DUCK & PORK! FRESH + FULLY INSPECTED MEAT!

His uncle's face was small from this distance, but the light from the sign helped. Louis could at least make out facial expressions. He waited for human traffic to pass out of his frame. "One two three!" He snapped. He snapped again and again.

"Are you done yet?" Uncle Bo asked.

"Almost! Are you capable of smiling?"

Uncle Bo forced a small grin that looked menacing.

"Go back to your normal face!" Louis snapped several more times before his uncle started backing away.

"Have a safe trip home!" Uncle Bo shouted, then turned and began to walk quickly.

Louis lowered the camera. "You, too!" he shouted, but he didn't know if his voice carried over the car horns, over the bustle of the sidewalks, and across the street as his uncle rushed toward a corner, around which he disappeared.

Louis called Grandma to report the finding.

"Having a good trip so far?" she asked.

"I spoke with the landlady."

"Go on."

"She showed me where Uncle Bo was," he said.

"Can I talk to him?"

"He's not here."

"Can I talk to him tomorrow?"

"I don't think I'll see him again. He wouldn't give me his phone number or address."

"Why not?" she asked. "Is he okay?"

There was a pause in which Louis considered telling her the facts of the past two days, and the words spoken by his uncle. He'd always been comforted by being able to separate factual truths from factual liberties, the way he'd differentiated Sung[2] from a person who'd truly existed.

People needed to know the truth, what they assumed indisputable. Ah-Kai's belief in Uncle Bo's death seemed to bring him peace, and Uncle Bo's belief that Sung[2] was his ancestor gave him satisfaction and something to write about.

Giving Grandma Uncle Bo's words would do her no good. They would bring no wisdom, no insight, and no knowledge worth the hurt they would cause.

"He's safe?" she asked.

"He's alive and in good health." Fact.

"Did he mention me?"

"He said he misses you." Factual liberty.

He didn't want to fill in the sentiment for Uncle Bo. He hated the word practical, hated more the notion of practical lying, and hated most the alternative of saying Uncle Bo mentioned her only to say she caused him physical pain. But liberty also meant freedom, in this case freedom from Uncle Bo's blame.

"He wishes you well." Factual liberty.

"I appreciate your help, Louis." Liberty.

The day after finding Uncle Bo, Louis received a call from the front desk. A package had been left for him.

Down in the lobby, he was handed a cardboard box. Inside was a thick stack of paper bound by a rubber band, a red envelope with gold characters printed on the front, and a note from his uncle:

Louis,

I'm glad we saw each other. I wanted to say something about your mother, but you didn't seem to want to talk about her. Before she died she used to send me a birthday card every year. It probably meant nothing special to her because she sent birthday cards to many people. She was very good at remembering dates and numbers.

Every year, she sent me a birthday card and a red envelope stuffed with money. The cards would be blank except for her signature, and your father's underneath hers. No message. Just their signatures and I knew it was really from her because your father never remembered my birthday when we were kids.

They (the cards and envelopes/money) were some of my favorite gifts because they were practical and understated. Nonintrusive.

I respected your mother and I had a lot of affection for her. I was very sad when I heard she passed away. This red envelope is the last one I received from her.

P.S. I also included the second part of Sung^2's life. It talks about how he got home. I thought you might want to read it.

The pages were all handwritten, like the first fifty-five pages Louis had received years ago. The story of Sung^2's journey back to China included ample descriptions of tatamis, shojis, and other Japanese home furnishings. It paid close attention to details of Japan's military hierarchy, peasant life, and farming tools in the thirteenth century. The story of Sung^2's return was told in forty-five handwritten pages, but could be summed up in a paragraph.

After the invading Mongolian fleet landed in Hakata Bay, Sung^2 deserted his ship and hid in the nearby woods. His desertion came right before the typhoon of 1281 struck the Mongols and destroyed their invading army. Left alone, he wandered Japan until he met the beautiful daughter of a high-ranking court advisor in Kyoto. They fell in love and wanted to marry, but her father disapproved. Her father convinced the emperor to banish Sung^2 from Japan, with the warning: "If you attempt to sneak the court advisor's daughter out of Japan with you, you will be beheaded." Sung^2 decided to leave without her. She begged him to take her with him, but he refused. He said, "I don't want to lose my head, but I do love you, like a fisherman loves a net bursting with carp." Then he hopped on a merchant vessel, returned to China, married a Chinese girl, and sired another Lum, who would sire another Lum and so forth until Melvin Lum was born, married Esther Hsieh, and sired Bo Lum.

The story reminded Louis of James Clavell's *Shogun,* which he hadn't enjoyed reading in high school. He'd found disappointingly improbable the premise of beautiful Japanese women from hundreds of years ago falling conveniently in love with a foreigner, one who probably couldn't speak their language correctly. A traveler, an immigrant, an illegal alien speaking with the accent and mastery of a native—that would be like Louis Lum speaking Cantonese well.

But maybe there was a thread of truth in that story. Louis recalled the letters Uncle Bo had written years ago, the details of his life in Hong Kong with Aunt Julie. One morning while on an acquisition trip for her museum, Aunt Julie had probably come across a scroll on which were written characters that told the story of a man named Lum Sung Sung.

After work she took a double-decker bus home, stuffed inside the lower deck with other tired, sweaty commuters, and eager to tell Bo of her discovery.

She got off after a few blocks and decided to hail a taxi instead, opting to spend a little more money for speed, privacy, and air-conditioning on a hot, humid day that reminded her of her honeymoon in Thailand.

On the ride home, she could see heat waves rising off the cement and trailing after the blackened exhaust of squealing buses.

She was surprised to find Bo already back. He usually returned a couple of hours after her, and today he was grinding whole bean coffee imported from Jamaica. The fine grinds let out a roasted scent that touched every corner of their tiny flat.

That night, they took a ferry out to Hong Kong harbor. Tall skyscrapers stood like lit candles in the distance, and the cool sea breeze washed the day's heat away from their bodies.

Afterward they went to a restaurant near Kowloon Bay and ordered steaks in black peppercorn sauce, a dish adopted from the British, and a bottle of red wine. He let her order because he still felt uncomfortable with his uneven Cantonese tones, and when she did order, she nudged his knee with hers and smiled, her way of signaling him to pay attention to her pronunciation, her way of teasing him.

Their stomachs full and their heads swimming with alcohol and the lush neon city lights, they strolled slowly hand in hand along sidewalks overflowing with travelers and lovers.

"You could be related," she said. "Would make sense. Another man who can't be bothered to stay in the place he was born."

Hours later they found their way back to their small flat in this crowded, mazelike, nocturnal city.

Lying in bed next to his wife, Bo Lum remembered the place he was born, and the thought of the thousands of miles of sea that separated his current position from that place sparked a bit of sadness.

He wanted to believe what Julie had suggested. He wanted to believe a man could leave family behind and find fulfillment somewhere else. He needed to because as much as he loved his family, they occasionally frightened him, particularly his mother, whose affection and need for affection manifested itself as a body-crushing weight, and he would rather remember her fondly from a distance than grow to resent her up close.

He sat up and watched Julie sleep, the gentle heave of her chest, and he felt light. He felt not like the awkward American foreigner she occasionally teased him of being. He felt right at home.

Louis picked up the red envelope. He wondered how much money his mother used to send Uncle Bo. Had it always been the same amount? Two twenties? A fifty? A hundred? Or a single dollar to deemphasize the money and emphasize the good health and blessings suggested by the gold characters printed on the envelope? How much had Uncle Bo's affection and respect cost? How much had his mother been willing to part with?

Louis didn't know because the envelope was empty, the money long since spent. It was fine. He didn't need to know. His mother would have wanted her gift put to use. That would have made her happy.

One Thousand Cigars
(1945)

When Melvin arrived home from the war, his face felt like sandpaper. It was gaunt and Esther touched the new hollows in his cheeks with shock and a sense of discovery.

He put down his green canvas bag, which jingled with shell casings, and hugged her. "I missed you," he said.

"Then you shouldn't have gone."

He hugged Dr. and Mrs. Lum, his brother, Phil, and his aunt, uncle, and cousins. They took him home and he slept for nearly two days straight. When he woke, he was quiet and Dr. and Mrs. Lum coddled him as if he was a newborn.

At dinner, they picked meat and vegetables for him, placing the food in his rice bowl until he said, "Stop it." He spoke with a new voice of authority, which was a very tired and hoarse voice.

After dinner, he'd say, "I'm taking a bath," and Dr. and Mrs. Lum would stop what they were doing and ask, "You need any help?"

They checked on him before he went to sleep, asking whether he needed a glass of water or more blankets. Sometimes, they'd touch his shoulder and say, "Sleep well," which wouldn't have annoyed Esther as much if she wasn't already lying next to him while they tucked him in.

She figured Melvin needed to live in his own head for a while, and decided to give him a week. She let him sit by himself in their bedroom or the living room. She didn't approach him for sex or conversation.

At week's end she asked, "Did you fulfill your duty to your country?"

He shrugged.

"You want to tell me what you saw in France?" she asked.

"No."

"Anything you want to talk about?" she asked.

"No."

"Are you going to be able to adjust to life here?"

"What do you mean?" he asked.

"Before you left, when I asked you a question, you responded with more than one word."

He kissed her on the cheek and said, "Good night." Then he turned out the lights.

She'd been sharing this three-bedroom apartment with his parents and brother in San Francisco's Chinatown since she married him. Space was expensive and the Lums didn't have much money. Dr. Lum, who'd been a doctor of either literature or medicine in Canton, had worked at a cigar factory and then a meat cannery after the cigar factory closed. He had one tweed suit he wore on weekends to show he was more than just a factory worker, which to Esther meant he was a man capable of wearing a tweed suit on weekends.

Mrs. Lum taught English in the local public school and Esther served as her assistant, earning a salary that wasn't enough to afford a new home. Esther's current home, this three-bedroom apartment shared by five adults, was too small. Her bedroom was just large enough to hold her bed. Her closet held her clothes, and Melvin's were folded and placed underneath the bed. The lack of space, underscored by Melvin's return, chafed her.

She lay awake that night next to her husband, who also lay awake, neither of them talking, and she remembered what her father used to tell her: "Don't forget you're worth one thousand cigars."

It was a bedtime story he'd told her as a child, and one which had brought comfort in its remembrance.

When she was born, all of Chinatown took notice because ninety percent of the population were men, eight percent were female prostitutes, and only two percent were unspoiled girls like herself.

The suitors began lining up outside her apartment the day her parents brought her home. Scores of men. Men of all ages, sizes, and shapes. Some had beards. Some didn't. Some had moles on their faces. Some had perfect complexions. All were desperate for the female companionship withheld from them by immigration laws.

"She can't even walk yet," her father told them, but they begged and pleaded for her hand in marriage, if not now, then fifteen years from now.

"They were trying to place reservations," her father used to say proudly. "Or they were coming on behalf of their sons. They offered me money. A lifetime cut of their salaries. They offered clothes. They offered to pay part of my rent each month."

Among the suitors was Dr. Lum, who rolled cigars at a factory and brought one for her father each night after work. Tied around the cigars were red ribbons her father slid off and hung over her crib.

Months passed and the accumulated ribbons formed a red spherical star that captured the light of the room's lamp.

"The smell of the leaves was so strong," her father would say, "it'd stay on my fingers for days."

This was true. She remembered Dr. Lum's hands, the stench of the leaves, and the yellow-brown stains they'd left on his fingernails and palms.

Sometimes when she was wearing a dress she thought beautiful and the sun lit her face and revealed her clear skin, she believed the story. Sometimes when she looked in the mirror and saw only a pale, scrawny girl, she didn't believe any of it.

There were suitors by the time puberty struck, but they weren't lining up around the block. A dozen fathers came on behalf of their sons. A dozen suitors. A dozen. Not the one hundred and twenty her father had sworn by. And one of the dozen was Dr. Lum, a thin man who sometimes brought barbecued pork buns for her and her mother. "He'd given me a thousand cigars by the time I promised to marry you to his son," her father often said.

Her husband would have been Phil, the firstborn, but he'd said he didn't have time for a wife. Dr. Lum had often complained about him, saying he loved alcohol and other pungent chemicals more than girls. "Alcohol is for drinking," Dr. Lum told Esther's father. "My boy uses it to make things explode."

Dr. Lum had wiry arms and loose flapping skin under his neck, and Esther wondered if he'd even been capable of rolling one thousand cigars. One thousand was probably her father's euphemism for one hundred, which was probably an exaggeration of ten.

Her father watched her wedding with the nervous excitement usually reserved for a high-stakes game of mah-jongg. During the banquet, he slapped her on the back and laughed cheerfully like she'd just produced the winning ivory tile from the crack in her ass.

After Melvin returned from the war, and faced with the vacant expression he offered whenever she asked a question, Esther often remembered her father's lie, the fairy tale he had passed off as history. Instead of stirring the imagination of all the men in Chinatown, she'd really just stirred the interest of Dr. Lum, who wanted wives for his sons and who'd probably given her father no more than five cigars.

How else to explain the situation she was in, lying next to a man who wouldn't talk or smile, a man with Popeye tattooed on his arm, a man who if unable to communicate normally with people because of something that'd happened in the war, had no one to blame but himself because everyone he knew and loved had told him not to go?

As she lay awake that night, Esther imagined herself, Melvin, and their yet unborn children spending weekends together in their own single house. A thousand square feet with a full-sized kitchen and three bedrooms. She wanted a new home away from the Lums and Hsiehs.

"War's over," she whispered. "Enough moping. You're getting a job—we'll each take two if we have to. We're moving out. Southern California's warm all year round."

Melvin didn't object. In fact, he didn't say anything. His eyes were shut and he continued sleeping, his breathing so soft she had to strain to hear it.

He mumbled something, then turned to sleep on his side, his back to her.

She took that as a yes and leaned her head into the gap between his shoulder blades. The indentation felt like a small cave for her face, and she was comforted by its steady warmth as she drifted into sleep.

Tripping on Benadryl with Ah-Mah
(2002)

Sonny woke to find himself alone. He usually dreamed about Mirla, the two of them lying on the couch. She'd lie on top of him and he'd cradle her in his arms. In this last dream he'd found Louis in the kitchen with a basket of fried chicken. The boy had held up a greasy drumstick and said, "This, Dad, is a leg!" He began eating, periodically stopping to wave the drumstick at him. "Hitting people will not make you feel better. Slapping Arnold Mannion didn't help, did it?"

When Sonny woke he realized he'd only slept an hour and a half. He usually slept no more than three or four a night. He needed a seven-hour sleep, which he hadn't had in a long time. The last thing he remembered before falling asleep was Ah-Mah whispering, thinking he was already out, "What do you know about romance?"

The TV and halogen lamp were off. He distinguished objects in the room by differing shades of dark. He got up and walked slowly to avoid bumping his knee into the coffee table and ramming his shoulder into the corner of the TV, which he sometimes did late at night, groggy from insomnia and wandering the house.

He went to Louis's room and opened the door a crack. He heard his mother's steady breathing inside. He went back to the sofa in the living room. It was two in the morning.

When he was fifteen, he'd imagined pleasant problems he and Mirla would have after they were married:

He turns pro and they move to Europe, where he wins mostly flat stages in the Vuelta a España, the Giro d'Italia, and the Tour de France. (He cannot feature himself winning the whole of any one of these races. Out of respect for legendary Tour winners like Eddy Merckx and Fausto Coppi, he cannot grant himself their accomplishments even in a fantasy.)

Upon returning to Orange County, he becomes the *Register*'s local sports hero. By this time, the French have dubbed him *Le Wheel-Man* and whenever he visits Paris, they hound him in the streets and shout, *"Le Wheel-Man! Le Wheel-Man!"*

The *Register* runs articles on his training regimen and dietary habits. He writes an advice column in the sports section called "Ask the Wheel-Man," in which he responds to husbands who get grief from their wives for riding too much, and kids who aspire to ride as well as him.

Under his column is a black-and-white photo of him posing in just cycling shorts, his chest smooth and his abs sharply defined. He receives love letters and marriage proposals from lots of women, which upsets Mirla. She says, "People only refer to me as the wife of the incredibly handsome and talented Wheel-Man."

He tells her, "Without you, my trophies would be meaningless," and brushes his hand across her cheek while looking over her shoulder at his three-feet-tall trophies.

She smiles, runs her hand across his abs, and says, "I never realized how hard and sculpted your body really is."

"I'm sorry my successes upset you," he says.

"I understand now. Thanks for clearing things up for me."

After they were married, they had problems that weren't pleasant:

She comes home from church. It's the afternoon. He's on the sofa watching TV. His god-given right. "Why don't you come with me next Sunday?" she asks. "No, thanks." "Don't you want to be in Heaven?" "No such thing." "How can you not believe in God?" "Doesn't exist." "Fool."

They don't talk for the rest of the day and he's angry she called him a fool. He watches TV, unable to pay attention to what's on, Mirla's words crackling like loud static against his skull—CometoHeavenCometoHeavenCometoHeavenCometoHeaven-CometoHeavenCometoHeavenCometoHeavenCometoHeaven-CometoHeavenCometoHeavenCometoHeavenCometoHeaven-CometoHeavenCometoHeavenCometoHeavenDon'tgotoHell-Don'tgotoHellDon'tgotoHellDon'tgotoHellDon'tgotoHell-Don'tgotoHellDon'tgotoHellDon'tgotoHellDon'tgotoHell-Don'tgotoHellDon'tgotoHellDon'tgotoHellDon'tgotoHell-Don'tgo . . .

He watches *Wheel of Fortune* and realizes he can't even answer something like "S_NGAP_ _E, Place" until the contestant buys another vowel. He thinks, Who is this woman telling me I have to believe in Jesus and potlucks? What happened to Mirla?

He went to the kitchen. He wanted to call Louis, but didn't want to disturb his vacation. He opened the drawers. A meat tenderizer was a useful tool. For tenderizing meat. He ran his fingers over the sharp protrusions, then put it down. He handled the silverware. Checked the plates and glasses. Opened more drawers.

"What are you doing?" Ah-Mah asked. She had light feet.

He turned to face her.

"You don't have any canned food," she said.

He noticed he was holding a can opener in his right hand. He put it down on the counter next to the sink. "I'm going to see Hersey Collins."

"To do what?"

"I don't know. I need to see him. He and I need to talk."

"Calm down," she said. "Take a deep breath."

"I'm calm. I have to go."

"Give me five minutes."

"What for?" he asked.

"Sit on the couch with me for five minutes."

He went back to the couch. Ah-Mah brought two glasses of water and a hundred-tablet bottle of Benadryl Allergy. "When I'm feeling emotional," she said, "I take some and I feel better in half an hour."

"I don't think Uncle Phil wanted his formula to control our moods," Sonny said.

"Take a couple with me."

"The effect only lasts a couple hours," he said. "After it wears off I feel more awake than before."

She handed him two tablets. "Two each."

"One's enough to knock me out," he said.

"We take the same dosage."

"One for me is the same as two for you," he said. "You have better tolerance."

"Fine." She took back one of his tablets.

"You first," he said. She popped the pills in her mouth and he put his index and middle fingers against her throat as she swallowed. Ah-Mah was a crafty woman and he respected her for that. "Stick out your tongue," he said. "Say ahhh."

She stuck out her tongue, raised it, lowered it, swung it left and swung it right. He was certain she'd ingested the pills.

"Your turn," she said.

He put the pill in his mouth. He had never told Ah-Mah about his surgery. When he was twenty-eight, he'd had all four of his impacted wisdom teeth removed. The extraction was performed by a stocky Romanian who kept wiping sweat from his forehead and blood from his scalpel, proclaiming, "This does not hurt! This is not even the beginning of pain!" as he sliced, drilled, and braced his knee against the side of Sonny's chair to yank, grunt, and pull.

The procedure had left four holes in the back of his mouth. Food often got stuck in these crevices of gum tissue, shards of apples, and peanuts that lingered hours after brushing.

He maneuvered the pill into his left bottom hole as he swung his tongue to reveal the upper right side of his mouth, then hid it in the right bottom hole while she scanned the upper left side. When she asked to check the bottom of his mouth, he guided the pill up into the spaces behind his molars.

She made him repeat several times. How far they'd come, from a time when she used to confiscate his candy to a time when she was trying to force-feed medication to sedate him. This was his mother at her most affectionate.

"Slower," she said. "Let me see all the way in. What are you hiding?"

"That's enough," he said. "You saw everything." He closed his mouth and moved the pill under his tongue.

He turned on the TV, waiting for a bit of time to pass before getting rid of the pill. If he rushed to the bathroom now, she'd know he was up to something. If he waited too long it'd melt in his mouth.

"I used to fantasize about winning stages in all three major bicycle races," he said.

"So?"

"It's hard to stay in peak form year-round, even for a superbly gifted athlete, which I was not."

"Okay." She studied his face.

"I was very arrogant," he said.

On the TV was an infomercial for an exercise machine. The spokeswoman, a thin but muscular blonde in red Lycra, spoke about the advantages offered by the contraption's series of adjustable levers, steel cords, and knobs while a big man rippling with muscles and wearing just shorts and sneakers performed leg curls, flexing his oversized quads and calves in the process.

"That piece of crap won't do a damn thing," Sonny said. "What a waste of money. All you need is a bike and a warm, clear day."

"Look at those muscles."

"They're just for show," Sonny said. "Too big. Not practical."

They continued watching the man, who was named Brad. After finishing his leg reps, he began pulling down on an overhanging bar attached to a set of weights.

"Look at Brad work those lats," the spokeswoman said.

"Nice lats," Ah-Mah said.

"What do you know about lats?" Sonny asked his mother as the spokeswoman talked about calories burned and time saved.

About ten minutes had passed. Sonny stood up.

"Where you going?" she asked.

"To take a piss," he said.

"You sure you need to go?"

"How can I calm down if you're constantly suspecting me?" he asked.

"I'm not suspecting you. I just don't think you need to take a piss."

"You're not helping me calm down."

"Fine. Be quick."

He locked the bathroom door behind him and spit the pill into the toilet bowl while pissing.

He came out and sat back down on the sofa.

"It's fine to have a healthy ego," she said.

"I've had a very, very unhealthy ego. I've been thinking of Mirla as my right leg. I used to think that was a compliment."

"You're my son," she said. It was a silly thing to say, as if being her son alone justified Mirla-as-leg as a compliment. She seemed to know it and waited for him to call her on it, which he didn't.

"I talked to Louis," she said. "Bo's doing fine."

"Good."

"Do you want to know where he met Bo?" she asked.

"Sure."

They met at a McDonald's. Louis ate cheeseburgers while they talked. Bo worked in a bakery. Bo was alive and that was good, and Sonny didn't care for the other details about the landlady and her family. He waited for the Benadryl to make his mother drowsy. At around the half-hour mark she leaned back against the sofa cushion and closed her eyes. Her breathing slowed.

He waited, didn't move, breathed as quietly as he could. He put two fingers under her nostrils and felt the gentle exhalation of air.

When he was certain she'd fallen deep into sleep, he went to his room. He needed a trip to see mountain ranges and rolling pastures. Tourist attractions. Things he hadn't seen before. Graceland and the Space Needle. A cross-country drive to see so many new things he wouldn't have room left in his head to think about Hersey Collins. Louis would understand.

He imagined sleeping seven consecutive hours in a quiet motel, the Do Not Disturb sign hanging on the door. He packed his clothes, half his records, and his passport. He packed his cell phone. He packed a toothbrush and a half-empty tube of toothpaste. Reading glasses. His watch. A framed photo of Mirla holding Louis when he was a baby. Then he tiptoed to the kitchen. He peeled several sheets off a yellow Post-it pad and stuck them on the kitchen table:

Louis,
Taking a trip. The house is all yours while I'm gone. I left half my records for you. Learn some culture. I'll write again when I'm settled down somewhere.

Ah-Mah,
Thanks for staying up with me. Went to see Hersey. Don't follow. I'll be gone before you get there. Don't worry. Won't kill him.

A Kind of Communion
(1987–1988)

Louis' father, Sonny, once visited Golden Harvest Baptist Church. It was a Saturday morning and Louis had been planning to spend the afternoon reading the dictionary when his father came to his room and announced, "Your mom's church is giving food to homeless people."

Louis was looking at the page beginning with "phenomenalistic" and ending with "philoprogenitiveness."

"Your mom asked us to stop by."

"I'm studying for the spelling bee," Louis said.

His father was standing near the doorway, his immense form blocking it. He looked over Louis's head at the far wall, at the bookshelf that held Louis's encyclopedia set and the dust-covered globe his mother had bought with the hope of improving his geography grade. "I understand," Louis's father said. "That would probably be a much better way to spend a Saturday and I won't force you to come with me."

"Okay. I'll see you later."

"You're coming with me."

"You said you weren't going to force me," Louis said.

"I thought you'd say yes." His father looked at Louis's dictionary with pity.

"I'd rather study."

"I understand," his father said, "but it's your mother. It's church." There was a desperate look in his eyes. "You can't just let me go alone. It'll be thirty, forty-five minutes tops. Then we'll come back and you can study all night if you want. Please."

"Fine," Louis said.

"We'll probably be helping them hand out food."

"Sounds fun," Louis said.

"You're not the only one suffering, kid."

On the drive over, Louis's father steered with his left hand and fidgeted with the radio with his right, changing from station to station.

"Dad."

"Yeah?"

"Can we stay on one station?"

"Having a hard time finding a good one."

"Okay, but can you leave it on one anyway?"

"Here." It was an AM news station and they listened to the stock index report the rest of the way to church.

They arrived to find the sidewalk outside the front entrance of Golden Harvest Baptist Church filled with people. Several long folding tables had been placed end to end, with food stacked on top—loaves of French bread, bricks of Cheddar and Monterey Jack cheese, cans of beans, and bottles of grape juice.

Louis's mother came outside and handed Louis a small green apron and a pair of white gloves. "Put these on and go give Beth a hand," she said. As he put on the apron and gloves, he noticed his mother was wearing a red bandana on her head and a pair of overalls stained with white paint.

"You look like Aunt Jemima," he said.

Louis's father elbowed him and said, "You look nice."

Louis walked to where Beth Carlson was handing out food

baskets to the people in line, most of whom were pushing shopping carts filled with rolled-up sleeping bags, tattered woolen coats, and gallon bottles of water.

"Nice to see you!" Beth said. "You look happy today."

Louis was frowning, but Beth said that to everyone she met. He stood next to her behind a table and she instructed him on what to do.

He picked up a wicker basket, stuffed it with bread and cheese, and handed it to a man with torn sneakers and dirty jeans.

"The juice," the man said, and Louis handed him a half-gallon bottle of grape juice.

Louis's parents were talking right in front of the church entrance, loud enough for him to hear.

"I spent a lot of time on it," his mother said. "Just come in for a few minutes."

"I'm here, Mirla," his father said. "Isn't that enough? I'll help Louis pass out food."

"Louis doesn't need help."

At this point, Louis's father looked at Louis, who smiled, not saying a word.

"I have to go in?" his father asked.

"Only if you want to," his mother said.

His father's face underwent a series of agonizing contortions before he finally said, "Fine. Let's go."

Louis's parents headed through the open doorway and into the church.

His mother had spent the past Saturday repainting Pastor Elkin's lectern, on which she'd also put a fresh coat of varnish, and she was eager to show off the results of her labor.

Louis knew his father wouldn't notice the lectern. His father never liked being in church. He would probably spend most of his time looking at the exit.

Sonny hadn't slept for two days. This was the first funeral he'd attended for an immediate family member and his back ached. He sat in the front pew thinking, How ridiculous for a man to end like this, a man who'd fought in a war, who'd lived fearlessly, moving from the comfort and familiarity of San Francisco's Chinatown to the middle of Orange County, a strange place filled with wide roads, acres of undeveloped land, and square, pristine suburban housing tracts. What a stupid thing it was, how unfair for this man to have been struck down by an ice cream truck while crossing the street in one of these supposedly safe suburbs.

Sonny looked at the blown-up black-and-white photo of his father, Melvin, dressed in a black suit with a white shirt and skinny black tie. His eyes were stern and his mouth an even, horizontal line. He had the expression of someone angry that he'd been killed by an ice cream truck. This thought made Sonny smile, though he didn't think it was funny. He couldn't help it. He'd been feeling strange all morning, like he wanted to cry, like he wanted to laugh, like he wanted to ride a hundred miles on his bike and just be left alone for a few weeks.

Mirla tapped his arm and mouthed, Are you okay?

Sonny nodded.

While the pastor delivered his message, the only thing Sonny could hear was Joplin's "The Entertainer," that annoying tune that blared unceasingly from the loudspeakers of ice cream trucks, and no doubt was playing on the one that hit his father.

After the pastor finished delivering his message, Bo came up to speak. Sonny felt constricted. Mirla and Louis sat to his left, and Larry, Helen, and their three kids sat to his right. His father's

friends and acquaintances sat behind him. The weight of everybody's presence seemed to push in on his chest, making it hard to
breathe. The fabric and wood of the pews gave off a strange
smell, like laundry detergent. He felt sick.

Bo looks so calm, Sonny thought. He looks trim and fit in his
suit. That's a nice suit, a blue so dark it looks black. Wonder if
he got it on sale. That's a damn good suit.

"My father was fond of aphorisms," Bo said. "I used to bring
my tape player out to dinner and he would feed it his pearls of
wisdom. He was particularly fond of saying, 'Cowboys who
clean their guns too often will lose gunfights.' I think he was
telling me not to masturbate too much."

There was scattered laughter. Sonny smiled at Bo. Bo smiled
back.

"My father rarely burdened my brothers and me with his
personal problems," Bo said. "Whatever troubles he may have
had in his life, whatever personal disappointments or tragedies,
he kept to himself and I've always respected him for that."

There was silence, and in this quiet Sonny felt his heart ready
to burst. He'd reached his breaking point. He didn't know he'd
been heading toward a breaking point, didn't know he'd been so
close, but here it was, his heart beating like a jackhammer, blood
throbbing through his temples, an overwhelming state of anxi-
ety, and the need to get the hell out of the room. He stood up.

Bo looked at him with a confused look.

"Sorry," Sonny said. "Keep going. It's a good speech." And
with that Sonny hurried out of the pew, past Mirla and Louis,
and ran down the aisle toward the exit.

Outside he vomited that morning's orange juice, eggs, and
hash browns onto the front lawn. Then he began coughing, bent
over, one hand on the church's wall for support.

Next thing he knew, Mirla was holding him, rubbing his back, and saying, "You're not going crazy."

He couldn't actually remember standing upright and moving toward her, and he didn't remember saying, "I'm going crazy," but he must have given her that response. What he did remember was hyperventilating in her arms and leaning on her for support.

The homeless people had scattered and leftover food dotted the tables.

Louis's parents came back outside and his mother handed him a loaf of French bread and a bottle of grape juice. "Take them home," she said. "I'll make garlic bread."

Louis's father looked like he'd just finished a tough math exam. "You ready?" he asked Louis.

"Yeah," Louis said.

"You can stay if you want," his mother said to him. "We're going to Pastor Elkin's house for music."

Pastor Elkin sometimes held Saturday afternoon music shows at his house. Accompanied by his wife on the electric keyboard, he'd belt out renditions of Air Supply's "Making Love Out of Nothing at All [Lord]," Hall and Oates's "[Lucifer is a] Man-eater," and other modified easy-listening standards.

"No, thanks," Louis said.

"Are you sure?" his mother asked.

"Definitely."

His mother walked them to the car. Louis put the French bread and grape juice in the backseat, then got in the front passenger seat. His father kissed his mother on the cheek, then got in the car. His mother watched as they sped out of the parking lot.

"So what'd you think?" Louis asked.

"She did a good job." His father scratched his head. "I really wasn't paying attention."

"My mind wanders when I'm in church, too."

"I'll never understand how you do it. Every Sunday morning."

"I just think about something else. I think about all the words I'll know later that day."

His father smiled for the first time all day. "Then let's get you home fast." He hit the pedal and they zipped sixty-five in a forty-five zone toward home.

Sonny and Mirla were waiting outside the church as the mourners exited. By now Sonny had dried his eyes and had resumed normal breathing. Mirla continued rubbing small circles on his back with one hand as Louis approached.

"Are you sick?" Louis asked him.

Sonny shook his head, afraid that if he tried to speak, the words would be accompanied by a new flood of tears. He kept his mouth shut tight.

"No," Mirla said. "Dad's just tired."

"Okay." Louis then ran to his cousins, saying, "Look at my tie. I did it myself."

The funeral director came outside and started counting heads. The mourners were to drive to Rose Hills Memorial Park, where Sonny's father would be buried. The train of cars would be accompanied by two CHP escorts.

"Nine cars total, including family and friends," the director told the officers.

Larry was going to drive Helen and their kids. Bo was going with Ah-Mah, and Sonny was supposed to drive Mirla and Louis, but Ah-Mah said, "Why don't you ride with Bo and me?"

Mirla said, "Go with your mother," and Sonny nodded.

The first CHP officer led the train out of the parking lot and the second rode behind it. Bo's car was the first in the group and Sonny kept his eyes fixed on the CHP motorcycle's brake light as his brother drove.

Ah-Mah sat in the back, quiet.

The radio had been turned off, the air conditioner had been set on medium, and the only sound was the flow of air from the vents.

Soon they were on the 605 Freeway heading north. Sonny hadn't even noticed getting on the freeway.

"I wanted to tell you two first," Ah-Mah said. "I didn't think Larry would care much, and it would be better if you told him anyway, Sonny."

"Tell us what?" Bo asked.

"Your father never killed anyone in World War II."

"Okay," Bo said.

"I just thought you should know," Ah-Mah said. "I want you two to have a truthful understanding of your father."

"It doesn't change my opinion of him," Bo said. "I always assumed it was a story anyway, all that talk of him fighting back the Nazis."

"He was a good man," Ah-Mah said.

"I know that," Bo said, and Sonny heard defensiveness in his brother's voice. "It doesn't change my opinion of him. But Louis and the other kids already believe Ah-Bah killed lots of Nazis."

"Well, it's up to you what you want your son to believe about his grandfather," Ah-Mah said to Sonny.

Sonny wanted to say he agreed with Bo, that his father's actions in war had no bearing on the affection he held for his father, but the mere thought of that black-and-white photo, accompanied by the memory of Joplin's "The Entertainer," quickened his heart and brought him close to that breaking point once again. He bit his lip.

Why not let Louis continue believing his grandfather had shot lots of Nazis? Wouldn't it only generate affection in the boy if he believed his grandfather had done heroic things in France?

"You need to puke again, Sonny?" Bo asked.

Ah-Mah caught the worry in Bo's face and poked her head up to take a look at Sonny's. "Are you sick?"

Sonny was breathing quickly and he fought to calm down. He squeezed his knee with his right hand. "I'm not going crazy."

"We didn't say you were," Bo said. "Do you want me to pull over?"

Sonny kept his eyes on the CHP officer riding so calmly ahead, the sun gleaming off the silver chrome of the bike's tailpipe.

"No. Keep driving."

"Are you sure?" Bo asked.

"Just keep going."

"Is this about what I said?" Ah-Mah asked.

"No," Sonny said. "Nothing to do with you."

As they drove by barren, brown hills that swelled along the right side of the freeway, Sonny wondered what effect the truth would have on Louis. Probably none. His son hadn't been fazed by the funeral proceedings, and had seemed more curious than grieved.

Sonny's father was dead, killed on a warm, quiet Saturday afternoon, and there was nothing in this world that could change that fact.

The CHP officer signaled right and diverted the train of cars toward the freeway exit. Sonny's eyes followed the officer, sitting erect and alert on his motorcycle. As the car approached the rising green pastures of Rose Hills, Sonny thought over and over, hoping repetition would make the wish reality, Let me never feel this way again. Never again.

Hersey Collins
(2002)

Sonny had always been touched by Louis calling him old bean. It'd been a term only his son used. Because of that, it'd been a term of endearment even when Louis was angry, as when Sonny refused to buy him a Nintendo game cartridge.

"Old bean!" Louis had said. "You're such a stingy old bean!" The memory of Louis standing in the Toys "R" Us aisle and refusing to move made Sonny smile. He was disappointed Louis had discovered the correct tone because old bean was, as Mirla had often said, such a nice touch.

It was selfish of him not to have corrected Louis, to have let the boy grow up using poor Cantonese for his satisfaction, to have avoided being called an old man.

He was now an old man visiting a young man, with butterflies in his stomach. He felt silly for being nervous, for this queasiness similar to what he'd felt on his first date with Mirla. He was confronting the man who'd killed her, and he felt like a fifteen-year-old boy picking up a girl. He didn't know what he'd say, how he'd stand, whether to put his hands in his pockets or not. Didn't know how Hersey would respond. It was three-thirty in the morning. He'd probably be sleeping.

Sonny gripped the wheel tightly and drove through quiet, empty streets. He knew the path to Hersey's well, having driven it in his head thousands of times. Hersey lived in a duplex in Garden Grove, where rent was cheaper than nearby Huntington Beach or Costa Mesa. Adult book stores and strip clubs had lowered property values.

He lived four miles away, a very short distance by car, a drive that was over before Sonny had even thought of turning on the radio.

It was a cream-colored building with dark brown shingles, with a front yard that was more dirt than lawn, and there Hersey Collins stood in a baby-blue bathrobe and green flip-flops watering the front dirt with a garden hose.

Sonny tooted his horn, as if to let a friend know he'd arrived. He felt stupid after he did it. He wasn't a friend and this wasn't a friendly visit. He got out of the car and as he approached, his shadow enveloped the young man. Sonny noticed the wideness of his own body. Because he used to ride so much, he'd become accustomed to taking in a high number of calories to make up for the calories burned. After he stopped riding, he continued eating the same amount without working off the excess—late night snacks of salty chips and ice cream had fattened him, given him a protruding gut and love handles that he pulled on when he was frustrated. Louis was right. He needed to lose twenty pounds.

"Why are you up?" Sonny asked.

"Mr. Lum," Hersey said. It sounded like a question and surprise covered the young man's face. Sonny didn't want him to be surprised. He wanted him to answer questions.

"Why are you up?" Sonny asked again.

"I don't know," Hersey said. "Sorry."

"Don't apologize," Sonny said. Why was he apologizing for being awake? He'd wanted more resistance from Hersey. A small part of him had wanted an excuse to get angry and fight, had hoped Hersey would say, What the hell are you doing here, you bitch-ass punk?

"I like to water my lemon seeds at night," Hersey said. His eyes were fixed on Sonny and the water hissed a small arc that ended at the front of his feet, where a puddle of water was collecting.

There were a few derelict weeds. No tree in sight. Just a square lot of dirt. Sonny kicked up a small cloud of it.

"I planted the seeds a week ago," Hersey said. "I'm hoping to grow my own lemons."

Sonny didn't know what to say to that.

"Free lemons," Hersey said. "Good idea, right?" He looked nervous. He dropped the hose and it made a small splash in the water puddle. "If you've come to beat me up, I won't fight back."

"Why won't you fight back?" Sonny asked.

"I won't."

There were bags under Hersey's eyes. He hunched. He would not fight back. It'd be like smashing a flea against a coffee table, Sonny thought. He'd only hurt his hand. "I'm too tired to fight," Sonny said.

"Sorry," Hersey said.

"For what?"

"For making you lose sleep."

"That's all?"

"And for everything," Hersey said.

"When you say you're sorry for everything, what do you mean?" Sonny asked.

Hersey looked confused.

"What do you mean?" Sonny asked again.

"I mean I fucked up and we both can't sleep as a result."

"You're right you fucked up," Sonny said. "You should have been driving a smaller car. If you'd been driving a compact, she'd be alive. Why were you driving a Land Cruiser? What the fuck did you need such a big car for?" He was breathing heavily, working up a sweat on his forehead, under his arms, and on his back.

Hersey's arms were glued along his sides and the blue sleeves of his bathrobe hung low, covering his hands.

He fucked up, Sonny thought. He admitted it. Sonny nodded at the hose, the head of which was now bubbling under the puddle it'd created. "Stop wasting water."

"Right." Hersey walked to the spigot at the side of the duplex and turned it off.

"You still at the hospital?" Sonny asked.

"I'm on leave. The ER rotations can be stressful."

"What do you do about money?"

"I work at a clothing store," Hersey said.

"Retail?"

"Yeah," Hersey said.

"You support yourself on that?" Sonny asked.

"I also temp."

"Finishing your residency later?"

"Maybe."

"So what do you do besides water dirt?" Sonny asked.

"I'm watering the lemon seeds."

"Right," Sonny said.

"I watch TV. Listen to music."

"What kind of music?" Sonny asked.

"You want to come in?" Hersey asked. "I can show you."

"Fine."

Potted plants filled the living room. There were Mexican heathers dotted with small purple flowers, long loping birds of paradise, and ferns. It looked like he'd robbed the Santa Ana Zoo's cow display of its flora.

"You want something to drink?" Hersey asked.

"Gin."

"I don't have any alcohol," Hersey said.

"Diet Coke," Sonny said.

"Diet Fuzz okay?"

"Diet Fuzz?" Sonny asked.

"It's orange soda."

"I don't want anything to drink," Sonny said.

Hersey went to his bedroom. Sonny inspected a plastic bin next to the TV. Inside were labeled bags that held seeds for basil, garlic, green onions, and red bell peppers.

"Amit recommended I grow things to relieve stress." Hersey returned with a stack of CDs. "Amit's my psychotherapist. Used to be my college roommate. Do you have plants?"

"You saying I need therapy?" Sonny asked.

"That's not what I mean." Hersey handed him the CDs.

Liz Phair. Indigo Girls. Aimee Mann. White women with long blond hair.

Sonny looked from the CDs to Hersey and back to the CDs. "Are you really black?"

"Both my parents are," Hersey said.

"Because this. What is this? Moody folk music?"

"I'll play you a song."

"No," Sonny said. "Wait here." He walked out to his car and returned with his only copy of *Straight Outta Compton*. He took a long look at it, at Dre, Cube, and Eazy, at their frowns, at the gun being pointed at the camera. He could use a break from hardcore. Maybe he should switch to more lighthearted fare for his vacation. Biz Markie's *I Need a Haircut* always put a smile on his face.

He handed the record to Hersey, who looked at it with fear and hesitation. "This is about your culture," Sonny said. "Your roots."

Hersey looked unconvinced.

"The struggle for equality and respect," Sonny said. "You know what I'm saying?"

"I grew up in Costa Mesa."

"You'll thank me," Sonny said.

"Thank you. I appreciate this. I was just wondering how I'd play it."

"With a record player," Sonny said.

"I mean I don't have one." He offered it back to Sonny. "If it's something you value, I'd feel bad taking it."

Sonny pushed it back. "Go to your parents' house and listen to it there."

"They're more into jazz."

"Listen to it and I'll forgive you," Sonny said. Look at him, Sonny thought, watering dirt in the night, listening to moody folk songs. He had such a misguided sense of what music should be. He needed recommendations, not a beating.

"You will?" Hersey asked.

"Will you listen to it?" Sonny asked.

"Yes. I promise."

"From beginning to end," Sonny said. "Don't skip any tracks."

"I won't," Hersey said. "I'll listen to this at my grandparents' house tomorrow."

Grandparents? Sonny thought. "Don't your parents have a record player?"

"They sold theirs," Hersey said.

"But they had one, right?"

"Yeah."

"Are they my age?" Sonny asked.

"How old are you?"

"Around fifty."

"They're about your age," Hersey said.

"Good." He was old, but he wasn't grandfather material yet. He turned and walked out the door. Hersey followed him to his car.

"Thank you for the record," Hersey said. "I promise I'll listen to it."

"You better." Sonny got in and shut the door. As he drove away, he checked the rearview mirror and saw Hersey waving, the sleeve of his bathrobe flapping. Sonny tooted his horn to say good-bye.

Melvin's Aphorisms
(1955–1987)

1) There's a time for eating and a time for crapping.
   Translation: Your child cannot stay with you forever. He has to grow up and move out.

2) A car runs badly with a flat tire.
   Translation: A wife should always agree with her husband in front of the children.

3) Possums will always hunt chickens.
   Translation: Germany and Japan should never be allowed to have a military again.

4) Kick a dying cockroach, and it will remain dying.
   Translation: Don't be a fascist. Let the boys ride their bikes around the neighborhood.

5) Cowboys who clean their guns too often will lose gunfights.
   Translation: Don't masturbate more than twice a day.

6) The son obeys the father because the father is the father.
   Translation: If you get your girlfriend pregnant, I will break your neck.

7) The higher the monkey climbs up the tree, the sweeter the grapes it retrieves.
   Translation: The harder one works, the sweeter the rewards.

8) Dry leaves crackle loudest.
   Translation: Grab Grandpa a beer from the fridge.

9) It's so hot I can fry noodles on my ass.
   Translation: It's so hot I can fry noodles on my ass.

10) In a knife fight, the guy with the machine gun wins.
    Translation: If a bully threatens you, hit him on the head with your three-ring binder as hard as you can.

11) Cannibals like their meat rare.
    Translation: ????

12) I can burp and fart at the same time.
    Translation: Leave Grandpa alone and go play in the yard.

Note: Aphorisms told to Esther (#1–4), Sonny (#5–7), and Louis (#8–12) between the years 1955 and 1987. Translations based on the context of the conversation in which the aphorism was stated, along with Melvin's declared meaning and what the listener believed the aphorism really meant.

A Departure, An Arrival
(1979-2002)

The year Louis was born, Bo left home to attend Berkeley. For Esther, every new arrival seemed to coincide with a departure, and her children were always departing.

A couple of days after Bo left, Melvin caught her crying on the concrete patio. He pulled up a chair next to her. He was chewing on a piece of bread smeared with peanut butter. "What are you doing?" he asked.

"You have nothing better to do than bother me?"

"Nope," he said. He sat there for a long time before finally saying, "There's a time for eating and a time for crapping."

She said nothing.

"I'm a poor substitute for company," he said.

She nodded and said, "Yes." Then she laughed. It was a tired laugh. Actually, it was more an exhale of grief rather than a laugh.

Melvin offered her a piece of his bread, and when she refused, put an arm around her shoulder.

It wasn't as bad a year as she'd expected. The year of Bo's departure, she and Melvin went to the movies twenty times. They ate out at least three nights a week. After dinner they settled on the couch to read the newspaper and drink tea, their arms and thighs pressing together as they shifted or poured more for themselves.

They made love fifteen times that year, which was fifteen more times than they had in the previous three and a half years. The first time, in the kitchen, they approached each other nervously like virgins. While she was drying the dishes, he put his hands on her hips and when she didn't resist, moved them away from the sink to the living room floor.

They started missionary style. He moved in counterclockwise circles above her for three or four minutes, stopping to catch his breath. She reversed their positions. She straddled him and set a slower, more proper rhythm, holding on to the loose skin above his hips for balance. They rocked together for another twenty minutes until he finished with a happy moan.

Later in bed he asked, "Wasn't that fun?"

"Better than reading the paper."

The second time they made love was after dinner at an Indian restaurant. They capped the night off with a bottle of Melvin's hundred-proof rice wine. The scent of tandoori chicken, curry, and alcohol seeped through his skin. He smelled delicious. She bit his neck and then touched the depressions her teeth had left in his flesh. He spanked her and when he saw the surprise on her face, said, "Felt like an interesting thing to do." She licked her lips. They clawed each other until their backs were red-streaked, as if they were punishing themselves for the years not spent making love, and fell asleep on the floor, their elbows and knees carpet-burned, their backs covered by a quilt.

When Esther woke, she found herself alone on Sonny's sofa. She saw his notes in the kitchen and her first word, uttered with anger, was, "Fuck!"

She felt like she was just cracking the door open to Sonny's life. She had hoped he would eventually share with her his music, show her the names of artists and songs the way she'd tried to share her music at the Lum family meetings, most of whom had listened to Billie Holiday with bored expressions, tapping the tabletop and yawning.

Louis had asked her to do one thing, to make sure Sonny didn't go to the home of that boy who'd killed Mirla. Where in his mouth could he have hidden those pills? She should not have let him piss alone. She hoped Louis wouldn't be too angry with her when he found out. He did his job in Hong Kong. He'd found Bo alive and well. She was the one who'd need to come up with an explanation.

Louis had the photos developed and was relieved to see that Uncle Bo's face was discernible. His uncle's brows were furrowed and his lips were sucked in as if he was in extreme pain, but proof was proof.

Louis wandered the streets at night. Red and white signs lit the Tsim Sha Tsui District to the brink of day. The air was warm and humid. Wild smells flooded his nostrils. Sewage from the alleyways. Barbecued pork from the all-night diners. Carbon monoxide from the taxis.

The heat of car exhaust swept his calves, and he was satisfied walking in his shorts and T-shirt. A lone white T-shirt among throngs of teenagers clad in black. The young here dressed like they were mourning, and why should anyone mourn?

Uncle Bo was alive.

This discovery energized Louis and propelled him through the city. He could see why his uncle held such fondness for Hong Kong. He liked the idea of ordering rice porridge at two in the morning. He liked the idea of young couples wandering the streets until dawn. He liked the old women hunched in front of their newsstands, shouting at him, "What are you staring at? Buy something or move along!"

Wal-Mart and Target were what he'd loved back home. He'd felt great joy in seeing the red bull's-eye shine in an Orange County night, signpost of a store where he could buy Benadryl, socks, and soda. The silver glitter and sparkle that rows of camera and jewelry shops produced in Hong Kong set off a similar contentment, the comfort of bright lights in the dark.

Each dusk his stomach knotted in excitement. Days he slept and nights he traveled beyond Kowloon to the New Territories and Hong Kong Island. Louis asked one driver if he had any hobbies and he said, "Horses." Louis asked where the horses were and the driver took him by the giant racetrack at Sha Tin. The driver gave him a tip, and the next day Louis lost about forty U.S. dollars on (not so) Furious Breeze.

He saw the Jumbo Floating Restaurant light up the waters off Aberdeen Harbour in red and gold. He decided not to take the boat out to the restaurant because the taxi driver had said the sight from afar was better than the seafood inside. "Where should I eat?" Louis asked, and the driver said, "I know a good place. You like Japanese food? It's called Yoshinoya."

After that, Louis learned not to ask for dining, betting, and any other suggestions from the drivers.

In the Central District, he saw The Center, one of the tallest skyscrapers in Hong Kong. It had a needle-like structure on top and was worth seeing just so he could tell his family and coworkers, I saw one of the tallest skyscrapers in Hong Kong and it had a needle-like structure on top. One of the benefits of traveling was having anecdotal things to say at parties and barbecues. It was both benefit and pretentiousness, and though he disliked pretense, Louis couldn't help thinking flat to describe an apartment and harbour to describe a harbor. Harbour was not more precise or accurate than harbor. A flat was just an apartment.

At Aberdeen Harbour he bought Grandma a steel necklace and his father a *Hong Kong!!* T-shirt. The old man had said he didn't want any souvenirs, but Louis didn't want to come home empty-handed.

Immediately after discovering Sonny's notes, Esther made a list of reasons for his successful escape attempt, but not one was satisfactory. Not one could she present to Louis and expect him not to be angry. They all boiled down to "Your father's tricky!" and, "I let him piss alone. Sorry." They all boiled down to her failure to watch over her own son.

The least she could do was make sure Sonny didn't hurt himself or that young man. She called Sonny's cell phone, but he didn't answer. She left a message. "This is your mother, you sneaky bastard. Call me. Don't do anything stupid like hit people. Don't drink. Drive safely."

Louis had given her Hersey Collins's address and phone number in case Sonny decided to go after him. "You can warn him that Dad's coming," Louis had said.

She called Hersey Collins. "Are you the man who ran over Mirla Lum?"

"Who is this?" he asked.

"Yes or no. I'm Mirla's mother-in-law."

"Yes. I'm sorry—"

"Did Sonny Lum visit you?" she asked.

"Yes, he just gave me—"

"Did he hit or threaten you?" she asked.

"No. He—"

"He left peacefully?"

"Yes."

"Was he drunk?"

"No."

"Did he tell you where he was going?"

"No."

"You're alive and in good health."

"Are you asking me?"

"You are, right?"

"I feel great. Thanks for—"

"Fine," she said. "Good-bye."

The night before his departure, Louis called home. Grandma answered the phone.

"I'll be back tomorrow," Louis said. "You and Dad doing okay?"

"We're fine."

"Good. I'll see you soon."

While waiting for his plane to take off from Chek Lap Kok Airport, Louis swallowed three Benadryl tablets. Two was the recommended adult dosage, but flying made him nervous. He fell asleep and woke to eat, and took three more and fell asleep again, waking to eat and falling asleep again—pattern repeated—until he landed at LAX.

Grandma met him outside the international terminal. She was alone.

"Where is he?" Louis asked.

"If I told you, you might have wanted to come home right away," she said. "I didn't want to ruin your vacation."

She explained what happened on the drive home. When they pulled up the driveway, she asked Louis if he was feeling fine.

"I'm tired," he said. The aftereffects from the Benadryl lingered. His mouth was dry and his cheeks felt numb.

The litmus test for how much he loved someone was how

much he missed the person after he'd left. Love was not vague. It was not a generic, all-inclusive term because he missed Will more than Grandpa, Connie more than Will, his mother more than Connie. And he missed his father very much while reading the old man's Post-its on the kitchen table.

"'Learn some culture,'" Grandma said, looking over his shoulder. "What kind of a good-bye is that?"

"It's in character."

"What does that even mean?" she asked.

He shrugged.

"Do you want to take a nap?" she asked.

He shook his head.

"You want me to make some coffee?"

"We have coffee?" Louis asked.

"I went shopping yesterday." She spooned grinds into the coffeemaker and asked about his trip.

He talked about Fei and her family, Jumbo Machinders, *Rose-Colored Fist,* and The Center. "The building has a needle on top," he said.

Grandma didn't seem to be paying attention. She seemed to be listening to the coffee drip. Whenever he finished a sentence, she said, "Good for you."

She'd been chewing gum anxiously since the drive home, and continued chewing throughout his vacation summary.

When he finished talking, she said, "That's interesting. Good for you." What she was really saying was, Please show me the proof.

He reached down and pulled the photos from his backpack. "Here."

She snatched them from his hands. "He's lost hair."

"Yeah." He looked at his father's Post-its. The old man had a rigid printing style. He wrote firmly, leaving dark square strokes on the paper. His P's were squared flags, and his O's were rectangular boxes. He wrote how a highway patrolman or an FDA official would write.

"He said he needs to be alone?" she asked.

"Yes. He's not ill. Not depressed. Just wants to be alone."

"He's always been like that," she said, not looking up from the pictures. "He hated company. Birthday parties used to scare him."

"Doesn't surprise me," Louis said.

"I mean his own birthday parties," she said. "They used to frighten him. He wouldn't be able to sleep the night before, not from excitement, but from the fear of everyone being around him."

"Then he's better off alone," Louis said.

"He said he missed me?"

"Very much."

"He looked skinny?" she asked.

"A little thin."

She nodded to signal that that was acceptable.

"Don't worry about him," Louis said. He pulled out the necklace from his backpack and handed it to her. He'd wanted to buy a more impressive souvenir, something with a trace of gold or silver, but plain stainless steel seemed appropriate for her. She thanked him and put it on.

That night Esther said to Louis, "I'll stay up with you."

He was watching TV in the living room. The sound was low, barely audible. "I'll be sleeping soon," he said.

"Your father said you don't sleep much."

"I'm getting ready for bed. Infomercials make me sleepy."

"Okay. Good night."

"It wasn't your fault with the Benadryl," Louis said. "He has holes in his mouth. He was probably hiding the pill in one of them."

"What?"

"The oral surgeon was a large man," Louis said. "Yanked out his wisdom teeth plus a big chunk of his gums."

"He never told me."

"He'll be back," Louis said.

"How do you know?"

Louis got up off the sofa and led her to Sonny's room. There he pointed at the records stacked on the floor next to Sonny's bed. "He only took half," Louis said.

"Maybe he only liked half."

"He left the standard." Louis searched for a record, found it, and showed it to her. It was made by a group called the Sugarhill Gang.

He put it on the record player, then sat on the floor, his back resting against the side of Sonny's bed.

"What are you playing?" she asked.

" 'Rapper's Delight.' "

"You like it?" she asked.

"No."

"You like any of his music?"

"Not at all," he said.

"Then why are you playing it?' "

"You've never heard this one. It's a standard."

Louis closed his eyes. By song's end he'd fallen asleep. She turned out the lights, shut the door behind her, and let the music play.

*　　*　　*

Grandma woke him, jabbing the cordless phone in his face. Louis was sitting against his father's bed. "Your dad," she said.

Louis checked his watch. He'd slept a couple of hours. He took the phone from her and she left the room. "Hello?"

"Louis. Have a good trip?"

"Sure."

"I hear Bo's alive."

"Yeah," Louis said.

"How's he doing?"

"He's fine."

"Great," his father said.

"Where are you?" Louis asked.

"On the I–15 to Vegas. I'm going to drive cross-country."

"What happened with Hersey Collins?" Louis asked.

"We talked. No fighting. I gave him *Straight Outta Compton*. He was listening to Linda Ronstadt."

"Linda Ronstadt?" Louis asked.

"Similar kind of music. Somebody named Indian Girls. Aimee Mann."

"I listen to Aimee Mann," Louis said.

"Great."

"Nice of you to give him the album."

"Yes, it was," his father said.

"How are you going to listen to your records?" Louis asked.

"I bought another player for the trip. I can listen in the motels."

"Does the bank know you're gone?"

"I took a leave of absence," his father said. "Are you done vacationing? You're welcome to stay in the house."

"I'll stay until you get back," Louis said.

"You can save on rent while you're there. Don't forget to pay the utilities. Cancel the cable if you want."

"Good luck in Vegas," Louis said.

"What I said about learning culture. Put down the Aimee Mann and start listening to what I gave you."

"Sure," Louis said. "Have a good trip."

There was a pause.

"I don't want you to worry about me," Louis's father said.

"Okay. I won't."

"I just want you to know that I fully intend to come home. I'm not going to drive off a cliff or cut my wrist. I don't want you to lose any sleep over me, and it just occurred to me that telling you I'm not going to kill myself probably makes you think I'm going to kill myself. But I won't. I promise."

Louis hadn't expected this. He didn't believe his father would kill himself, and he didn't want to say anything that might encourage him to. He searched for an appropriate response. *"Ngóh seun néih."* he said.

Louis rarely used Cantonese with his father, but this was a simple, basic phrase he remembered from those *How Are You, Willy Lau?* Cantonese instructional tapes. It was a response Joseph often gave after his father provided some interesting fact about the woolly mammoth or Komodo dragon. It translated into I believe you, but the word for believe, *seun,* could also mean trust.

"That's good," his father said. "Good to hear."

Larry Redux
(2002)

Grandma Esther moved out after Louis arrived, and he returned to work at the hot rod magazine, to his life in Orange County, to fact checking, to wide streets, empty sidewalks, ample parking, and Target shopping centers, their red rings lighting up the nights.

Finding Uncle Bo alive had been a relief, but it hadn't convinced him that Death no longer stalked his family. Uncle Bo's presumed drowning and his appearance at McDonald's had been Death's way of saying, "Made you look." It'd been His sick joke, and Louis stayed wary. He kept on his toes. He continued to wait seven seconds before crossing a street on a green. Continued to order cheeseburgers from fast food chains without the patty. Continued to worry about his father crashing his car on a highway.

In his father's room were two framed black-and-white photographs. The first was of Grandpa Melvin. Wide face, small eyes, sharp nose, a row of teeth. Narrow black tie against a white shirt and black jacket. He was smiling like he'd been forced to at gunpoint.

The second photo showed Tupac being wheeled out on a gurney after being shot five times in the building that housed the studio of rival rapper Biggie Smalls. His head, neck, and chest wrapped in white gauze, Tupac had managed to raise his middle finger high up in the air, saluting not just the photographer, but Death itself.

A week after arriving in Vegas, Louis's father sent him a letter. Attached to it was a five-dollar bill. "I'm up five," his father had written. "Least I'm not down."

That night, Louis dreamed of Jesus in the corporeal form of Max von Sydow standing in one corner of a boxing ring. He stripped off his white robes to reveal a chiseled torso. He smiled at the audience: Louis's mother and father, Grandma Esther, Uncle Bo, Aunt Julie, Uncle Larry, Aunt Helen, Mick, Will, and Connie. They were hooting and shouting, "Kick his ass, Jesus!"

A puff of smoke appeared in the other corner and from it emerged Death in the corporeal form of Grandpa Melvin, holding a machine gun and grimacing in his black jacket and tie.

Death threw the gun out of the ring and roared at Louis's family. They booed him.

The two combatants touched gloves in the center of the ring. There was no referee. Jesus had on boxing trunks and Death kept his suit on. After the bell rang, the two men circled each other while Louis's family hollered, "Go Jesus!"

The Son of Man unleashed a spin kick that landed square on the left side of Death's face, and followed with a punch to the Adam's apple.

This wasn't boxing. It was kickboxing.

Jesus kneed Death in the midsection and threw an uppercut that sent Death crashing to the mat. The bell rang again to signal the end of the bout.

Jesus spit out his mouthpiece, raised his arms, and said to the Lums, "Love one another!"

"This is a dream!" Louis shouted. He began laughing. He

couldn't stop. Jesus noticed him laughing and said, "Are you laughing at me?"

Louis couldn't stop laughing even as his family began shouting at him to shut up and Jesus began floating toward him, shaking a gloved fist.

Louis ran for the building's exit, pushed open the double doors, and woke.

His pillow was soaked through with sweat and the back of his neck was hot. He went to the kitchen. He poured a glass of water, tossed in two ice cubes, and pressed the glass against his neck before drinking out of it.

On his way back to bed, he stopped by his father's room. Grandpa's photo made him nervous. He stared Death in the eyes and said, "I don't believe in you." He said it again—"I don't believe in you"—then hurried out of the room.

Two weeks after arriving home, Louis received a call from Mick, who spoke with excitement in his voice. "Come over. Yeah, right now. You aren't creating Benadryl."

When Louis arrived, Mick invited him in and said, "Meet the latest addition to our family."

The new Lum was a Pembroke Welsh corgi, a small creature with long foxlike ears and the stubby legs of a footstool.

"This is Larry," Mick said.

"After your father?"

"It's a good name."

"I don't mean it's a bad one," Louis said.

Larry barked and raised a hind leg.

"No!" Mick bent down and shouted in Larry's face. "Pee outside! Pee outside!" The dog whimpered and Mick chased him into the backyard.

Louis followed.

"I'm making lunch," Mick said, nodding at his grill. He put two steaks on and slathered them with barbecue sauce while Larry peed. The dog began barking at a bird singing from the top of a fence post.

"I've cut down my workout schedule," Mick said. He said he'd also been seeing less of his old college buddies because he wanted to spend quality time with Larry.

"What do you do?" Louis asked.

"Play catch. Eat dinner together." Mick had found a day care center for Larry during the afternoons, complete with a two-hour exercise program at a local park, vitamin-supplemented meals, and weekly massages.

"You eat together?" Louis asked.

"Every night at seven-thirty."

"You don't start without him, or let him start first?" Louis asked.

"It'd be rude to start without waiting for the other." Larry lost interest in the bird and settled down at Mick's feet, whining for food. Mick pulled a doggie treat from his shirt pocket. The snack was reddish brown and shaped like a small bone. He bit off half and tossed the other half into Larry's waiting jaws. Mick chewed happily.

At the end of January, four months after arriving home, Louis received a postcard from Montreal. He'd been receiving post-cards from places including Portland, Houston, Des Moines, Brooklyn, and Providence. The old man had driven east across the country and then headed north into Canada, where he'd spent Christmas and New Year's Eve at ABC Seafood in Montreal's Chinatown. "Good thing about Chinese joints—

they're always open," his father wrote. "I'm going to Vancouver next. Be back in April."

Vancouver was in British Columbia. It was north of Orange County. It wasn't directly north. If one drew a straight line from Orange County up through Canada, it wouldn't intersect Vancouver, but it'd come close, much closer than to Ottawa, Toronto, or some other city on the other side of the continent.

Louis knew which direction the old man was going. He hoped he got there safely.

The Dance of Good Fortune
(2002)

Every Chinese New Year Grandma Esther brought flowers to Rose Hills Memorial Park, where the Orange County Lums rested. The last time Louis had been there was for his mother's burial, and the time before was in '94 for Connie's. This year Grandma asked him if he wanted to go with her.

"Probably not," he said. He avoided that place unless a Lum was being buried, in which case he had no choice but to go. This year, Mick also wanted to go and encouraged Louis to come along. "I bought a dog, you found Uncle Bo," Mick said. "Good signs. Time to unburden your soul. Confront your fears. Visit Rose Hills."

"I don't know," Louis said.

"We can have lunch after," Mick said.

"I don't want to go."

"I'll treat."

"I really don't want to go," Louis said.

"I'll pick you up at eleven." Mick suggested Seafood Cove in Westminster for lunch, and Grandma approved. Lion dancers were going to assemble in front of the restaurant, as they did every February to usher in the new year.

Rose Hills occupied fourteen hundred acres, much of which consisted of rolling green hills. The place had always seemed like a slice of Pastor Elkin's Heaven, even back when Uncle Larry was buried.

Then Louis was ten, holding Connie's hand. She was seven, young enough not to understand the obligation to grieve like her two older brothers, who were busy walking their mother up and down the hills of the memorial park.

Louis had been charged by his parents with watching Connie for the afternoon. She was polite and a good conversationalist.

The two of them had been impressed by the tall stone archways that formed what Connie called "the ribs" of El Portal de la Paz, one of several mausoleums at Rose Hills. Outside was an enclosed garden with bright daisies and tulips. In the center of the garden was a gushing fountain.

"This architecture's patterned after the Spanish missions," Louis had explained, to which she said, "Cool."

He showed her a casket catalog he'd grabbed from the front office and they talked about what they wanted to be buried in.

"I want a bright yellow mahogany one," she said, "so when I'm dead I can shine like the sun."

He wanted to say nobody would know or care what color the casket was after it'd been buried, but the prospect of a yellow one made her so happy he didn't want to dampen her mood.

"What kind do you want?" she asked.

"Something traditional. Brown all around. Oak with a grained light finish. Square corners. Crepe interior."

"Cool," she said, looking at the garden. She ran outside and picked some flowers.

After she died from that poisonous cheeseburger bought at that fast food restaurant, Louis did two things. He vowed to never again patronize any of the restaurant's seven thousand worldwide locations, and he resolved to get for Connie the casket of her dreams.

He explained to Aunt Helen that Connie had wanted a bright yellow casket. Aunt Helen made him swear he was telling the truth. He swore.

At the service Louis approached Connie's open casket thinking, I got you what you wanted.

His father led him up the steps.

In the movies the dead looked exactly as they had in life, and Louis had expected the same with Connie.

Her cheeks were sunken, her jaws bony protrusions. Her closed eyes bulged from their sockets and her skin was unnaturally white, bright as copier paper. "I want to go," Louis said. He began shaking, not from fear or grief, but from anger because he knew this was how he'd always remember her. This was the last and lasting image Death had given him of his cousin, and he was furious. "I want to go now," he said. *"Now."* His father grabbed his wrist and half sprinted with him out of the church.

He'd always regretted running away and felt a pang of shame now as he planted the bouquet of chrysanthemums in the receptacle above her plaque. He stood, ready to leave. He'd already visited his mother's plaque, Uncle Larry's, Will's, and Grandpa's. The process included walking, searching ("I'm sure it's right over that hill," Grandma had said a couple dozen times), and moments of observation (a minute of silence followed by the planting of the flowers followed by another minute of silence), and had taken two and a half hours. The Lums were buried in different locations across Rose Hills' fourteen hundred acres, and finding them all had been tiring. Now that they'd finished their visitations, the day was almost over and Louis couldn't wait to have lunch, go home, and shower.

Off in the distance, Mick tossed a yellow Frisbee to Larry, who leaped over a headstone to catch it. Mick barked his praise, pulled the Frisbee from Larry's jaws, and tossed it again. Standing behind Louis, Grandma said, "No sense of dignity, that one. Acts more like a dog than the dog."

Louis drove to the restaurant, Grandma sitting next to him and examining the photos of Uncle Bo under the sunlight.

"Dude could use some Rogaine," Mick said from the backseat.

"Just hope it doesn't happen to you," she said.

"Whatever," Mick said, but a few minutes later Louis caught him checking his hair in the rearview.

A small crowd had formed around the restaurant's entrance, which faced Westminster Avenue. Louis stood next to Grandma and Mick. They were on the outskirts of Little Saigon, home to the largest Vietnamese community outside of Vietnam, right in the heart of Orange County.

As a child Louis had come to this area often with his parents, lunching on four-dollar bowls of pho and French-style Vietnamese sandwhiches stuffed with pâté, beef, cilantro, and pickled carrots. Now gawking at the lion dance preparations with the rest of the crowd, he felt like a tourist again.

There were four lion costumes, one green and three red. The lions had a head and butt section each controlled by a boy in a white T-shirt and jeans. One man assisted the dancers with putting on their costumes. Another set up a ladder and climbed it to tie a string of firecrackers and a head of lettuce over the restaurant's front doors. A third man set up two large cylindrical drums off to the side while the boys stretched their legs, their Nikes visible underneath the sides of the lion suits.

Saangchoi, depending on the tone, meant either lettuce or make money. The head of lettuce the green lion would devour signified good fortune. The red envelopes the assistants would pass out to the restaurant's customers for them to fill with money were intended to buy good fortune. Good fortune was also brought about by the dance, which began when the two drummers started pounding a beat with thick wooden drumsticks shaped like cigars.

The boys shimmied under the lion suits, reminding Louis of the family meeting years ago when Mick shook and twisted to Grandma's James Brown album. Mick had especially enjoyed the song about having ants in his pants and wanting to dance.

"In China, the dancers can balance themselves on top of poles and do flips," Grandma said as the lions swept past her.

"These dancers are twelve," Mick said.

"The ones in China are eight," Grandma said.

Mick held Larry's leash, the dog sitting quietly at his feet.

The lions snaked into the restaurant in single file while the two drummers continued pounding away, creating vibrations that shook the ground.

Mick yawned.

The lions came back out and the green one climbed the ladder over the restaurant's entrance. The boy's hand poked through the gaping jaws and pulled the head of lettuce into the lion's head.

Back on the ground the boy shredded the lettuce, throwing pieces out of the mouth. The lions shimmied some more and then backed away from the entrance.

A man with a cigarette lighter stepped forward and lit the string of firecrackers, which looked like a belt of bullets. He ran back to stand with the crowd.

Everyone plugged their ears.

The firecrackers exploded, snapping and popping.

Louis turned around to check on Grandma and saw Larry, startled by the commotion, jump up and bite Mick on the ass. Surprised, Mick dropped the leash and Larry ran into the street.

The cars added to the crackle of the firecrackers. Bleeping horns filled the air as Mick chased after Larry, who was heading toward the concrete center divider that separated the eight-lane street.

Mick pursued in zigzag fashion, stopping, starting, stopping again to avoid getting struck.

Let them live, Louis thought. If they made it across safely, he would balance all the losses he'd suffered with this twist of good fortune. He would learn not to fear that portrait of Grandpa. He would order burgers with the patties. He would not hope and not wish, but expect his father to return safely from his trip. He would measure this moment against all the deaths, and take hope in it.

The firecrackers spent and their loud popping stopped, the crowd turned to gawk at Larry and Mick dodging cars on the opposite side of the street.

"Larry!" Mick shouted. "Fuck off!" he shouted at the drivers who were honking their horns, screeching to full stops, and shouting at him to get off the road.

"Stupid idiot," somebody next to Louis whispered.

Louis turned to tell that person to shut up and saw Grandma, who said again, "Stupid idiot. So stupid." Her voiced carried affection and worry. She took his hand and squeezed it.

When both dog and man made it safely to the other sidewalk, she exhaled and let go of his hand.

The dog hesitated. He poked his nose up in the air and sniffed. He looked at Mick fifteen feet away and then in the other direction. As Louis and Grandma watched, Larry trotted back to Mick, who bent down with open arms to receive him.

Grandma shook her head in disbelief, and Louis understood that she'd been by his side the entire time, seeing everything he'd seen.

Acknowledgments

From the beginning Lance Uyeda, John Doan, and Robin Page provided constant friendship and encouragement, believing in my work when I often didn't.

Michelle Latiolais read more drafts of this novel than anyone should have to. Her dedication saved Bo Lum and her faith in the book was inspiring.

My agent, Dorian Karchmar at Lowenstein-Yost Associates, took a chance on me, and her enthusiasm and optimism provided me with a much needed second wind. My editor, Gillian Blake, asked me to spend more time with my characters and not to shortchange their lives, and the book is better for her contributions. My thanks also to Marisa Pagano, the rest of the staff at Bloomsbury USA, and Virginia McRae for their help.

Dr. Alvina Leung gave good counsel and had to convince me on more than one occasion that I didn't actually have a brain tumor. Dr. Peter Le has been a stalwart friend through the years, and is a constant source of beautifully bizarre stories.

Thanks to Geoffrey Wolff for welcoming me into the UCI writing program, and thanks to Arielle Read for helping me get through it.

In the program, Terence Mickey introduced me to many fantastic stories and novels I probably wouldn't have found on my own, and Mary Waters offered valuable advice and lessons on practicality.

NOTE ON THE AUTHOR

Chieh Chieng was born in Hong Kong and moved to Orange County, California, at the age of seven. He graduated from the creative writing program at the University of California, Irvine, and has been published in *Glimmer Train*, *The Threepenny Review*, and the *Santa Monica Review*. He is twenty-nine years old.

NOTE ON THE TYPE

The text of this book is set in Linotype Sabon, named after the type founder Jacques Sabon. It was designed by Jan Tschichold and jointly developed by Linotype, Monotype, and Stempel in response to a need for a typeface to be available in identical form for mechanical hot metal composition and hand composition using foundry type.

Tschichold based his design for Sabon roman on a font engraved by Garamond, and Sabon italic on a font by Granjon. It was first used in 1966 and has proved an enduring modern classic.